Girlfriends

Keri turned and reached behind her. "I've got something for you. A little pressie. Here!" She upended an envelope and scattered a sprinkling of small objects across the floor.

"Ooh!" Lily pounced. "Badges!"

I peered, short-sightedly. (I was trying to train my eyes to manage without beastly glasses.) "Boys R Us?"

"Cool!" Frizz giggled. She snatched one up and pinned it onto herself. Lily did the same.

"Well, go on!" said Keri. There was just the one badge left; she flicked it towards me. "This girl in my class, Adriana? Her dad made them for her. It's what he does; makes badges. Well, and other things, too, I guess. She's got a whole load of them, all different colours."

Mine was a blue one; quite pretty. I picked it up and pinned it on. "What's it s'posed to mean?" I said. "Boys R Us...what's it actually mean?"

Also by Jean Ure
in the Girlfriends series

Girls Stick Together!
Girls Are Groovy!
Pink Knickers Aren't Cool!
Boys Are OK!

Orchard Black Apples

Get a Life
Just Sixteen
Love is for Ever

ORCHARD BOOKS
338 Euston Road, London NW1 3BH
Orchard Books Australia
Level 17/207 Kent Street, Sydney, NSW 2000
First published in 2009 by Orchard Books

ISBN 978 1 40830 301 6

A CIP catalogue record for this book is available from the British Library.

1 3 5 7 9 10 8 6 4 2
Printed in Great Britain

Orchard Books is a division of Hachette Children's Books,
an Hachette UK company.

www.hachette.co.uk

Boys

R Us

JEAN URE

ORCHARD BOOKS

Chapter 1

"Fries," cried Lily. "I want fries!"

"OK." Frizz nodded, and made a note on her writing block: *Lily, First Course, Fries.*

I said, "You're not *really* going to have fries on the menu?"

"Why not?" said Keri.

"Cos they're bad for you!"

"Not in small amounts," said Frizz.

"I can't eat them in small amounts! They're like chocolate, and fudge... You get started and you can't stop!"

"You mean, *you* can't," said Keri.

It's true, I can't. Show me a plate of French fries and I'm like a horrible greedy guzzling thing. But I'm not the only one! "You have to have a sense of responsibility," I said.

"Speak for yourself," said Keri. "Look, can we just get on with things?"

"Yes." Frizz sat, pen poised. It was a Saturday afternoon a few weeks into the spring term and we'd all met up at Keri's place. Frizz was working out her menu for when she was a world-famous chef and had her own restaurant, the Green Gourmet. She'd told us all to pick our favourite dishes.

"Well?" She looked across at Lily, who was, as usual, sitting on the floor doing stretchy things with her legs, slowly unfolding them and lifting them up to her head. "What are you having to go with the fries?"

"Mm…" Lily considered. She now had one leg hooked round her neck. Sometimes I seriously think that girl has bones made of rubber. "I'll have…a whammyburger! *Double* whammyburger. Followed by sticky toffee pudding and pistachio ice cream – oh, and a huge big gluggy strawberry milkshake. Yum yum!" She licked her lips. I nearly licked mine, too. I adore strawberry milkshakes!

"Honestly," said Keri, "that is just too *utterly* gross."

"And you wouldn't eat all that anyway," I added. "Not when it came to it." Lily is a dancer and is just *so* careful about her food. The school she goes to, which is a ballet school, is extra-super-strict. No one must get too fat, and no one must get too thin. They are all weighed and measured every single week! So there is just no way anything gluggy or sticky would ever be allowed within *sniffing* distance.

"I can dream," said Lily, unhooking her leg.

"Not about whammyburgers." Frizz said it sternly. "I'm certainly not having those on the menu. Not having *any* kind of burger. Choose something else! I could do a nut loaf, if you like."

Keri said, "Yuck! Puke! Spare me!"

"Nut loaf's too healthy," said Lily. "I want something disgusting. Something that'd make Miss Diamond's eyes fall out!" Miss Diamond is the teacher that has the obsession with weighing and measuring. They are all absolutely terrified of her. "Something with megabyte calories," said Lily, her eyes gleaming in anticipation. "All fatty and sugary and sick sick *sick*!"

With grave dignity Frizz said, "Nothing on my menu is going to make anyone sick. But I could do you something like almonds and aubergine in a creamy sauce."

"That'll do," said Lily. "Cream'd send her screaming up the wall!"

"You still wouldn't eat it," I muttered.

"Well, that's all right," said Lily. "I'll let you have it, instead."

That scared me; I know how easily I fall prey to temptation. "I can't have gluggy stuff," I said. "I'm on a diet."

"*Again?*" said Keri. "You're always on a diet! You know they never work."

"That's because I never stick to them. I'm too weak-willed!"

"Diets aren't good for you, anyway."

"No, they're not," said Frizz. "You have to learn to eat sensibly. What are you going to choose?"

"Oh." I wafted a hand. "I'll just go for a salad and a bit of fruit."

Keri thumped on the floor with her fist. "*Bor-ing!*"

"It's not very challenging," agreed Frizz, "but if it's what she wants—"

"It is," I said, "cos it's healthy. If I even just so much as *look* at a chip I swell up like a balloon!"

"That's because you don't get enough exercise," said Keri. She, of course, is this mad sports fanatic who likes nothing better than thundering up and down a muddy playing field in the pouring rain, whacking at a hockey ball. "If you just got out and ran around a bit, you wouldn't have this problem."

"Excuse *me*," I said. "I take Bundle out *at least* four times a week."

"Why not seven?"

I roared, "Cos my brother's s'posed to!"

"But do you *run*?"

"No," I said, "I don't. Dogs run: people walk."

Keri looked at me, pityingly. She is not tiny and slender like Lily, but she is most terrifically *lean*.

"Anyway," I said, "come on! It's your turn."

"Yah! OK. Well, I shall have new potatoes with *fresh* green beans and a side dish of tabooly."

Pardon me???

"And to follow I shall have krem brooly." Well, that's what it sounded like. Lily and I exchanged glances. Trust Keri!

I waited for Frizz to say, "*What?*" but she didn't seem fazed; she was writing, quite calmly. I peered over her shoulder. Under "Keri" she had written, "*First course, new potatoes, green beans, tabbouleh. Pudding, crème brûlée.*" She not only knew what they were, she even knew how to spell them! Frizz never ceases to amaze me. She may not be any good at maths or science, or English or French, or any of those things that teachers get so worked up about, but there is almost nothing you can tell her about food and cooking. She's a genius!

"So what is this stuff?" said Lily, jamming her other leg behind her neck. "This taboulee stuff...what's it supposed to be?"

"It's really just a sort of salad," said Frizz.

Hah! I shot up, triumphantly. *Salad*.

Angrily, Keri said, "It's not just ordinary salad! It's made with bulgur wheat."

Lily peered out from under her leg. "Did you say *vulgar* wheat?"

"Yes, cos it's not just an ordinary salad," I reminded her. "It's obviously an extremely *rude* one!"

"Oh, for heaven's sake! You are *so* unsophisticated," said Keri. "All except Frizz," she added, graciously. "She

13

is really the only person one could take anywhere."

There had once been a time when Frizz would have glowed at such a compliment coming from Keri. She used to be so unsure of herself, so pathetically eager not to be left out, always scared of Keri and her sharp tongue. Then she discovered her gift for cooking and didn't care anymore what Keri had to say about anything. She was going to be a chef just as Lily was going to be a dancer, whereas me and Keri still didn't have the faintest idea what we were going to do with our lives. It had given Frizz simply masses of confidence. She is my very best and oldest friend, so naturally I was pleased for her; but I did sometimes have the uncomfortable feeling that maybe I was now the odd one out.

Lily unhooked her second leg and began on her arms. First in an arch over her head, then one of them out to the side, then the other to the other side, then round to the front. It would have looked ridiculous done by anyone else, even Keri, who is so terrifically athletic, but I don't think Lily could look ridiculous if she tried. I do sometimes envy her, being so slim and graceful. I just know that I'm going to end up like Mum, who is a beachball!

"OK, so we can't be taken anywhere." Lily smiled, dreamily. She never really pays any attention to Keri; she has known her too long. "What's this other thing you're going to have? This krem thing?"

"It's French," said Frizz. "It means burnt cream. And I shall *definitely* have it on the menu!" She beamed at Keri, who sat back, looking satisfied.

"Glad to be of help. By the way, you guys—" Keri turned and reached behind her. "I've got something for you. A little pressie. Here!" She upended an envelope and scattered a sprinkling of small objects across the floor.

"Ooh!" Lily pounced. "Badges!"

I peered, short-sightedly. (I was trying to train my eyes to manage without beastly glasses.) "*Boys R Us?*"

"Cool!" Frizz giggled. She snatched one up and pinned it onto herself. Lily did the same.

"Well, go on!" said Keri. There was just the one badge left; she flicked it towards me. "This girl in my class, Adriana? Her dad made them for her. It's what he does; makes badges. Well, and other things, too, I guess. She's got a whole load of them, all different colours."

Mine was a blue one; quite pretty. I picked it up and pinned it on. "What's it s'posed to mean?" I said. "Boys R Us…what's it actually mean?"

All three of them turned to look at me. They always seemed to be looking at me, these days. Like I was some kind of weird specimen in a pickle jar. Frizz giggled again. Keri said, "You have to be joking!"

"No, I just meant…what's it for? Is it advertising something?"

"You could say that," said Keri.

"A shop, or something?"

Frizz stifled another giggle.

"Not a shop," said Keri.

"A band! Is it a band?" I thought that was quite a neat idea. "I wouldn't mind advertising a band," I said. "But not if it's just a shop."

Huffily, Keri said, "Look, if you don't want it, give it back. I'll find someone who does."

"No, I want it," I said. "I want it!"

I like badges; I have lots of them. I have BAN ANIMAL EXPERIMENTS, which I happen to totally agree with, and I'VE BEEN TO OTTERWORLD, which I actually haven't (though I'd very much like to), and I LOVE ANIMALS (which I do!) and STOP THE BLOODY WAR, which I also agree with. I don't think wars should even be *started*. So if ever anyone comes up and asks me why I'm wearing some particular badge I can always tell them, cos I *know* why I'm wearing it. Otherwise you just look stupid.

I tried explaining this to Keri. "See, they're like a kind of statement, like stopping war. It's a *statement*. But if someone asks why I'm wearing a badge that says Boys R Us, I don't know what the answer is!"

"You don't know why you're wearing it?"

"No, cos I don't know what it means!"

There was a silence. They were all staring at me again.

"O-mi-god," said Keri.

Frizz had gone into more giggles. She never used to

16

laugh at me. She was the one that got laughed at. She said, "Polly, you are just so funny sometimes!"

I said, "Why? What's funny? I don't see what's funny!"

"Well, I ask you," said Keri. "Who wants to go round making statements all over the place?"

"She can't help it," said Frizz, coming to my rescue. Or I *thought* she was coming to my rescue. "She's a boffin. They're all boffins, where she goes."

She meant the High School. They were always going on at me about it. It wasn't fair! *I* hadn't chosen to go there. It was Mum and Dad, making me sit the stupid scholarship. I hadn't even wanted the scholarship! I'd actually done my best to fail. I *would* have failed if it hadn't been for pride getting the better of me at the last minute. I failed the maths bit OK, no problem! I didn't even have to try to fail maths, it came quite naturally. But then I had to write a poem and I got carried away and did eight whole verses, and they gave me a scholarship and Frizz and Keri have never let me live it down. Lily was the only one who didn't keep getting at me and calling me a boffin. *I hate being called a boffin!*

"Seems to me," said Keri, "anyone who doesn't know what Boys R Us means has to be practically brain dead."

"Or from another planet."

"Or old. Like really old," said Lily, hunching her shoulders and letting her mouth droop open. "So old they're out of it."

"And then you wouldn't want to tell them anyway, in case they might be shocked. Like, f'r instance, you wouldn't want to tell your nan," said Frizz.

"I could tell mine," said Keri. "'Cept I wouldn't have to, cos she'd *know* what it meant...that we're into boys in a BIG WAY!"

"Hurrah!" Lily whizzed round on her bottom.

"You'd better believe it," said Keri. "Did I tell you guys I'm going on a date this evening?"

"With who?" said Lily.

"Wait for it...Damian Whitchurch!"

Lily squealed. Frizz squealed. So I squealed, too.

"That's the one you fancied last term," said Frizz.

"Yup! When he was going out with that ghastly Barbie doll from Year 9? Emily *Smythe*? Puke!"

"So what happened?" Frizz settled herself comfortably on one of the big puffy cushions that lay scattered about on the floor. "Did he junk her?"

"Well, I couldn't see her junking *him*...I mean, Damian Whitchurch?" Keri went into a mock swoon. "Hunk from heaven!"

"How many out of ten?" said Lily.

"At least fifteen!"

Frizz squealed again. I gave a small squeak.

"So how about you lot?" said Keri. "Who's got a love life? Frizz!" She nudged at her. "You still all lovey-dovey with Darren?"

Frizz nodded, bashfully.

"They're practically an old married couple," said Lily. "Ah, look, she's blushing!"

Frizz's cheeks had turned a bright happy pink, like candyfloss. She didn't really mind being teased; I think she actually quite enjoyed it. Unlike me! I tend to get easily embarrassed. It is very *embarrassing*, getting embarrassed. When Keri switched her attention to me, saying, "And Polly's still going out with Rees, right?" I instantly turned into this huge overripe tomato.

"Now *she's* blushing!" cried Lily.

"What's going on?" Keri leaned towards me, eager for secrets. "Are you an item?"

I didn't know. Were we?

"Is that why you're blushing? Have you been up to things you shouldn't be?"

I said, "No, of course we haven't!"

"Rees wouldn't," said Frizz. "He's not that sort of boy."

Keri cackled. "They're all that sort of boy!"

"Not Rees." Frizz shook her head. "He's sweet."

Keri pulled a face, like, *how can a boy be sweet*? "Too much of a boffin for me," she said.

"Well, but so's Polly a boffin, as well!"

"True," Keri chortled. "It's obviously a love match… bags I be bridesmaid!"

By now my cheeks were practically bursting into

flames. To pay her back, I said, "You can be a bridesmaid if you really want, but you'll have to wear pink." I know how Keri feels about pink. She reckons it's girly.

"Puke!" She clapped a hand to her mouth and made loud vomiting noises. "I don't wear pink for anyone!" She turned to Frizz. "You're not going to have pink, are you?"

"I'm not going to have bridesmaids at all," said Frizz. "I've already decided. It costs too much money and my dad couldn't afford it. I'll probably just get married in a registry office."

I thought to myself what a noble and selfless act that would be. "I think I might do the same," I said.

"Not me!" declared Keri. "I'm going to have the full thing. How about you?" She leaned across and prodded at Lily, who seemed to have gone into some kind of trance. "You going to have bridesmaids?"

"Haven't really thought about it," said Lily.

"No, well, of course you mightn't get married at all," said Keri. "You might be too dedicated to your dancing… too busy flying about all over the place. Rome today, Paris tomorrow…you'll hardly have time to breathe!"

"But I'll still have lots of love affairs," said Lily.

"You bet! You'll be known for them. You'll always be appearing in things like *Hello!* magazine… *The world-famous ballerina, Lily Stubbs, with her latest boyfriend.*"

"I've told you before," said Lily, "I'm changing my name. You can't have a dancer called *Stubbs.*"

20

"All right," said Keri. "So what are you going to call yourself?"

"Something romantic."

"Such as what?"

"I thought maybe…" A hint of pink appeared in Lily's cheeks. "Something foreign. Lily…da Souza? Lily…. Dugard? Lily…"

"Dugard. That's cool! *The world-famous ballerina, Lily Dugard, with her latest boyfriend…Shane O'Malley!*"

Lily shrieked in outrage. "I wouldn't be seen dead with Shane O'Malley!"

Shane was a rather thug-like boy who'd been at primary school with us. He'd always had a bit of a thing about Lily.

"So who d'you want to be photographed with? Give us a name, give us a name!"

"I dunno." Lily hunched a shoulder. "Joel?"

"Joel who?"

"Joel anybody!" Lily sprang to her feet and danced like quicksilver across the room. "It's just a name I picked at random!"

Keri said, "Hm…" and gave her this look. The special Keri look which says, *There's something you're not telling us.* But Lily won't ever talk if she doesn't want to. Not even Keri can make her.

"It's a nice name," I said.

"It may be a nice name," said Keri, "but *who does it belong to?*"

Whoever it was, Lily wasn't saying. But as the three of us, her and me and Frizz, walked back down the hill together later on, Lily gave one of her little twirls and said, "Boys *Are* Us, aren't they?" She didn't wait for an answer; just went whizzing off across the road to catch her bus, leaving me and Frizz to ponder what her secret could be.

Chapter 2

"Something's going on," said Frizz, as we crossed the road to our own bus stop. "I think she's fallen for someone!"

"Probably someone at school," I said.

"Another dancer. Must be! Can't see her going out with anyone normal," said Frizz.

I giggled at that, but I knew what she meant. Lily is just, like, totally dedicated to her dancing. Dancing is the only thing she wants to do, and dancers are the only people she knows. Apart from me and Frizz and Keri, of course, but we have been friends since primary school.

"She's never really had a boyfriend, has she?" said Frizz. "Not a proper one."

I agreed that she hadn't, though she certainly could have done, if she'd wanted. There were loads of boys who would like to go out with Lily; I sometimes think she has more boy appeal than any of us, even more than Keri.

She is also by far the prettiest. Keri is tall and dramatic-looking, with bright red hair which foams and froths. But although she is hugely attractive, she is not exactly pretty. Neither is Frizz. In fact, Frizz is what people tend to describe as *homely*, meaning a bit plain, I suppose, if I am to be honest. But not in a way that would put anyone off! Frizz may not be drop-dead gorgeous, but she is always friendly and has this really nice smile – especially since she was allowed to take the brace off her teeth. That was definitely an improvement.

As for me, I am just boringly average and ordinary. And kind of *round*. I am not yet a beachball, like Mum, but I have this utterly ridiculous face like a squishy bun, not helped by the fact that I have to wear glasses. I hate wearing glasses! I take them off whenever I can, but I couldn't really walk round the streets without them, as everything goes all blurry and I would probably bump into lamp posts and knock myself out. I do so wish Mum would let me have contact lenses! I would have bright green ones, as I think green eyes are just *soooo* seductive. Keri has green eyes; clear and sparkling, like seawater. In her own way, she is quite striking, I suppose. But Lily is what Mum once called *enchanting*, with her bright glossy hair, jet black, and her tiny heart-shaped face. Boys just seem to melt at the sight of her. Even that yob-like Shane at primary school used to go a bit gooey. But up until now, it was true, Lily had never actually had a real boyfriend.

"*Joel…*" I tried the name out loud. It sounded good! I wouldn't have minded a boyfriend called Joel.

"Well, we shall see," said Frizz.

I said, "Yes, we shall await developments." And then, as casually as I could, I said, "So what are you doing this evening?" Hoping against hope that she would say "Nothing" and ask me if I'd like to stay over. I hadn't stayed over with Frizz for *such* a long time! "Are you seeing Darren, or…?"

"I'm going round his place," said Frizz. She blushed, contentedly. "We're trying out new recipes!"

"That sounds exciting," I said, doing my best not to sound disappointed and probably just succeeding in sounding horridly sarcastic. I hadn't meant to sound sarcastic. But I ask you! Who would want to spend their Saturday evening trying out recipes?

Eagerly, Frizz said, "We're working on our cookbook. Darren's doing the meat dishes, I'm doing the veggie ones. When we've finished we're going to publish it on the internet."

I made a vague gurgling sound of encouragement.

"We have to try everything out first, though, make sure it works."

I said, "Well, yes, you wouldn't want to poison people."

"We wouldn't *poison* people! We just want them to have a good eating experience." A bus lumbered into

25

sight and we stuck our hands out. "How 'bout you?" said Frizz. "You seeing Rees?"

I shook my head. "He's playing in some stupid chess tournament." I followed Frizz up the stairs and settled down next to her in the back seat. "He's obsessed by it," I said. "He told me the other day he'd even been playing chess in his sleep."

"I sometimes do that," said Frizz. "I dream that I'm cooking things. I cooked a whole three-course meal one time!"

I looked at her, glumly. "That means you're obsessed, too." But that was all right because so was Darren. They could obsess together. I, on the other hand, was not into chess and never could be as I simply don't have that kind of brain. I said so to Frizz and she said, "Still, you could have gone and watched…I mean, if it's that important to him."

"How can you watch chess?" I said. "Nothing happens!"

"You could have watched *him*. I'd go and watch Darren, if he was in a cookery competition."

"That's because you're interested in cookery. I'm not *interested* in chess. He keeps on about teaching me, but I just know I wouldn't be any good at it."

"You could always try," said Frizz. "It's nice if you can share things."

I sighed and said, "Yes; I s'pose."

"Well, but it is," said Frizz. "It means you can do things together."

I said, "We *do* do things together. I just don't want to play chess!" And then I stopped and thought about it and said, "What d'you reckon Keri does with her boyfriends?"

Frizz pulled a face. "I'd rather not know!"

"She has so many," I said. "I can't keep up with them."

"They can't keep up with her," said Frizz. "She obviously wears them out."

"But she can always seem to find a new one from somewhere! Imagine what it would feel like," I said, "being the sort of person who could get any boy they wanted, practically. Just looking at them and going, *Zap! I'll have that one.*"

"Who would you zap?" said Frizz.

That was easy. "Evan Quincy!"

"You really fancy him?"

"Don't you?"

"He's OK. Not really my type."

"No, well, of course, you don't appreciate his sort of music," I said. Not meaning to be superior or anything, but Frizz's taste in music is seriously uncool. "Who would *you* zap?"

Frizz stood up and pressed the bell as we approached her stop. "Wouldn't zap anyone...happy with what I've got!"

27

"*Bor-ing*!" I said; but she was already on her way down the stairs. I slid across to the window and waved. Frizz waved back. Then she mouthed up at me, "Boys R Us!" and tapped a finger on her badge. I nodded, and stuck up a thumb. Boys Were Us. Of course they were! How could they not be? I was into boys in just as big a way as everyone else. Except...I did sometimes miss the old days, when it had just been the four of us, Lily and Keri, me and Frizz, without any complications.

I wouldn't necessarily have wanted to be back at primary school, even though it had felt so cosy and such a comfort, going round in our own little gang, all hating that bossy Jessamy James and her showy-off friends. But I'd grown up since then; I quite liked being twelve. Most of the time. I probably wouldn't have wanted to go back to my first term at the High School, either, cos of not knowing people and being pounced on almost immediately by this girl Lettuce who kept clinging like a damp leaf and didn't want me to talk to anyone. Plus there was poor old Frizz, all by herself at Heathfield, being bullied by Darcie White and Melanie Philpott (Jessamy James's showy-off friends) and feeling deathly miserable.

We'd all tried so hard to stay together. In Year 6 we'd even taken an oath, vowing not to be separated. But in the end we'd got split up and sent to different schools, which at first we'd absolutely hated. Well, me and Frizz had hated it; I'm not so sure about the other two. I've always suspected that Keri just loved being a weekly boarder at her posh school in Hastings right from the word go, no matter how much she said she missed the rest of us. Keri is just, like, *the* most sociable person; she adores being the centre of attention and racing round with a whole crowd of people. As for Lily, she didn't care where she was or who she was with so long as she could dance. Me and Frizz were the ones that found it most difficult, but after a bit we managed to make new friends – *school* friends – so that by our second term it was all starting to work out really well.

I remembered how we all used to meet up every weekend, just like we'd promised we would when we were still at primary school. *We'll be friends for ever and ever.* It was such fun! We used to take it in turns, my place, Keri's place, Lily's place, Frizz's. We'd chat and gossip and share what was going on in our lives. We were as close as we'd ever been! Now we only met, like, about once a month, and it was always round at Keri's (cos of her having her own sitting room) and all we ever seemed to talk about was boys. Even if we started off with other stuff, like Frizz's menu for when she opened her restaurant, BOYS was how we inevitably ended up. Every single time. I wouldn't have minded, cos I mean I was just as interested in boys as anyone else, except I did sometimes feel they rather got in the way. It was because of BOYS we hardly ever seemed to do things together anymore. Instead of staying over on a Saturday evening with Frizz, for instance, I now (mostly) went out with Rees, while Frizz did things with Darren. Exciting things, like cooking…

Oh, but that was nasty of me! Cos it obviously *was* exciting, for Frizz. She loved cooking and she presumably loved Darren, so there wasn't any reason for me to be all snooty and superior. Darren might only rank about three out of ten, but what did that matter? He and Frizz were happy together.

I reached my stop and clattered noisily down the stairs. Clattering made me feel a bit better; less inclined to self-pity. I knew things had to change; they couldn't stay the same for ever. *We have to move on.* That's what people always say. Politicians, and people. I just wished we could move a bit slower, so I wouldn't notice! That was all.

When I got home, Mum demanded to know whose turn it was to take Bundle out. I said that it was Craig's (which it was). Mum yelled upstairs to him. "Craig! Are you going to take this dog for his walk?"

Craig's voice came honking back: "I haven't got time!"

What did he mean, he hadn't got time? "It's your turn!" I shrieked.

"I'll do it tomorrow."

"In that case you'll have to do it Monday, as well!"

"Yeah, OK. Whatever."

But he wouldn't; I knew he wouldn't. He is almost two years older than me but he is just *so* irresponsible. "He'll find a way to get out of it," I said to Mum. "He always finds a way to get out of it. It's not fair!"

"It's not fair on Bundle," said Mum. "We only got him on condition you'd both look after him."

"I do look after him! But it's *not my turn.*"

Mum sighed, and bellowed back up the stairs. "CRAIG! It's not your sister's turn. Stop what you're doing and take this dog out immediately!"

We heard a distant honking, then Craig appeared on the upstairs landing. He shouted, "Bloody hell, I'm trying to get ready!"

Mum didn't even tell him off for swearing, which I think she ought to have done. Instead, in a helpless sort of way, she said, "He's going on a first date with someone. He wants to look his best."

I stood there, mute. Bundle sat in front of me, wagging his stumpy tail and gazing up, his big doggy eyes full of trust.

"Do it this once," begged Mum. "I'll make sure he takes his turn tomorrow. And Monday. That's a promise!"

I muttered savagely about people making promises they couldn't keep, but I stomped into the kitchen, snatching up the lead, and Bundle bustled after me, so joyously that I hadn't the heart to be cross. Poor little dog! It wasn't his fault. I walked him up to the park and went all the way round and back across the middle and down one side and up the other and then all the way round again, just to show Mum that *one* of us was capable of keeping their word.

By the time we got back we'd been out for almost an hour and a half. Mum was really pleased. "That was an excellent walk," she said. "Thank you, Polly. *Craig will now do it two days running.*"

Craig said, "Yeah, yeah. Whatever."

"He better *had*," I said venomously.

"Bloody hell!" Craig did this thing he does, this stupid maddening thing, clenching his fists and drumming them on top of his head. "How many times have I got to say it?"

"He swore!" I turned, and shrieked it at Mum. "He swore at me!"

"Craig, don't swear at your sister," said Mum. "Don't swear at anybody. *Will the two of you please just stop it?*"

There are times, she is always telling us, when we get on her nerves. Well, my brother gets on mine.

"You look ridiculous, anyway," I said. He did, too. He'd gelled his hair so it stuck out in spikes, and he was wearing these really baggy jeans all wrinkled up round the ankles. They were *so* big and baggy he couldn't even

32

walk properly – he had to waddle like a duck. I said, "Quack quack quack!" and rocked to and fro in front of him. Craig's face turned a deep beefy red.

"Ignore her," said Mum. "There's absolutely nothing wrong with the way you look. I'm sure if I were a young girl I'd find it a real turn-on. Polly, that was mean! Your brother's got a very important date."

I said, "Humph! Pity any poor girl goes out with him."

"Pity any boy goes out with you," retorted Craig.

"Snotnose!"

"Pimple face!"

"P—"

"CRAIG AND POLLY!" Mum's voice came thundering across the room. "Just knock it off! Your dad will be home any minute. He doesn't need all this after a hard day's work."

We both slunk off, sullenly, in opposite directions. I knew I'd been mean, cos it's horrid telling someone they look ridiculous when they're about to go off on a date. Even Craig. I would just curl up and die if anyone did that to me. I suppose it was that I was jealous. Well, and mad, too, cos of him not taking Bundle out when it was his turn. But mainly it was jealousy. Everyone was going out except me! And maybe Lily, though as Frizz had said, *something* was going on even for her. For all I knew, she could be seeing this Joel person. It would be typical of Lily not to tell us till afterwards; she can be quite secretive.

But I didn't have any secrets! I was stuck indoors all by myself on a Saturday evening cos *my* boyfriend preferred to go and play chess. Nobody else had boyfriends who wanted to play chess!

I had a sudden last-minute idea and galloped upstairs to use my mobile in the privacy of my room, where Craig's great flapping ears couldn't eavesdrop.

"Chloe?" I said. Chloe is my best friend at school. We don't see each other outside so much, but we do sometimes. "I just wondered," I said, "if you're doing anything?"

"You mean, like, right now or later on?"

I said, "Later on. Feel like coming over?"

"I can't!" Chloe gave a little squeaky giggle that turned into an apologetic snort. "I'm seeing Rick."

I said, "Who's Rick?"

"This boy that's a friend of my cousin? The one I told you about?"

I was silent, trying to remember.

"The other day? I said my cousin might fix me up with a date?"

"Oh. Yes! Right. I'd forgotten."

"We're going out as a foursome."

"Right."

"I can't really ask you to come, cos I mean…"

"No," I said, "that's OK." I wouldn't have wanted to, anyway. Not on my own.

"Tell you all about it on Monday," said Chloe. "See ya!"

I said, "Yeah, see ya."

Slowly I ended the call and wandered back downstairs. Craig was studying himself in the hall mirror; Mum was reassuring him.

"Honestly, pet, you look fine!"

I shoved past them, a bit rudely, without bothering to say excuse me. *I* ought to have been the one Mum was reassuring. *I* ought to have been the one getting dressed up! I thought dismally that I was obviously some kind of freak.

The doorbell rang and Craig shouted, "That'll be Darcie! Her dad's giving us a lift."

I broke out into prickles. When he said *Darcie*...he surely couldn't mean *the* Darcie? I turned in a panic, looking for somewhere to hide, but Craig had already lunged at the door and yanked it open, and omigod, there she was, Darcie White, all done up like a daffodil, or some kind of egg yolk, bright puke yellow from head to foot.

She screeched, "Polleee!"

I said, "Darceee!" Craig looked at me and scowled.

"I'm off now," he said to Mum.

"Well, have a good time," said Mum. "Enjoy yourselves."

As she closed the door behind them I said, "That made my eyes hurt!"

"It was certainly a bit bright," admitted Mum. "But with her colouring she can get away with it. Do I take it you know each other?"

I reminded Mum that she'd been at primary school with me and was a friend of the dreaded Jessamy. "She used to bully Frizz something horrible when they first went to Heathfield."

Instead of agreeing with me that that made Darcie a pretty naff sort of person, Mum said, "Are you *still* referring to Dawn by that stupid nickname?"

"She doesn't mind," I said. "She used to, but she doesn't now." Not since she'd become an item with Darren and got all confident. "She's changed," I said, trying to keep a note of regret out of my voice and not quite succeeding.

"She's just growing up," said Mum, "that's all."

She put her arm round me as we went through to the kitchen, where we found Dad waiting for us. He had obviously come in through the back door as Craig and the Egg Yolk had gone out of the front. He said, "Hello, Poll Doll! Not out on the razzle?"

Primly I said, "I'm having a night in."

"Not seeing Rees?" said Mum.

I told her that he had gone to play in a chess tournament.

"Couldn't you have gone to cheer him on?"

I said, "It's not a football match! Anyway, I don't know

36

the first thing about chess."

"I'm sure you could learn."

"I don't want to learn!"

"It's a brain game," said Dad.

"Well, Polly's brainy," said Mum.

"True."

"She'd probably be quite good at it."

I groaned, inwardly. Any minute now and she'd start on about me winning the beastly scholarship. Yup! There she went.

"Anyone that can get a free place at the High School…"

I knew Mum only did it cos she was proud of me. I suppose I was, too, just a little bit, in spite of having tried my best to fail. I was proud of the poem I'd written! I think I'm quite good at writing poetry. If being a poet were a career, same as being a teacher or a doctor, it's definitely what I would choose. Unfortunately Mrs McPherson, our careers teacher, says you can't make a living from it. She adds, however, that this shouldn't stop anyone from trying.

"Always aim high," is what she says. "Never be scared to pursue an objective."

So that is what I am doing, I am pursuing an objective. In the meantime, *unfortunately*, I have to do battle with stuff such as geometry and algebra that I simply DO NOT UNDERSTAND. It is like being weighed down by a huge sack of potatoes. Everyone having all these expectations, like I was some huge great brainy boffin. Which I am not! Sometimes I just feel like curling up with Bundle and reading a good book; by which I mean the sort of book you can relax with, not the sort we so often have to do at school, where it is all hard work and *what is the author trying to say here* and *what is the author trying to do there* until you just give up caring. I like books where I can get to know the characters and they become my friends. Maybe that's what I would do tonight; I would go up to my room and cuddle with Bundle and read. And omigod! How sad was that?

Dad had been washing his hands at the sink. He turned, cheerfully, as he reached for the towel. "So how about old Frizzpot?" he said. "What's she up to, these days?"

Before I could mumble that Frizz was trying out new recipes with her boyfriend, Mum had stepped in to rescue me.

"I've had an idea," she said. "Why don't we all go up the road for an Indian meal? I can't remember the last time we had a curry!"

I said, "What about all this stuff you've just cooked?"

"Oh, that'll keep!" said Mum. "Don't worry about that. Come on! Let's splash out for once."

"I'm game," said Dad.

"Polly? You fancy an Indian?"

I said OK cos it would have been ungracious not to. Mum was trying really hard; she obviously felt I needed cheering up. I do so hope that when I have kids – *if* I have kids – they won't turn out to be wimps like me!

Chapter 3

I woke up the next morning full of guilt and remorse, thinking to myself that if I really cared about Rees, if I really *really* cared, I would have made an effort and gone to watch his stupid chess game. And that was another thing: I oughtn't to call it stupid. Just cos *I* was stupid and couldn't understand it. Like Dad said, it was a brain game. Probably I ought to think myself lucky to have a boyfriend who enjoyed playing chess instead of just wanting to rush around in a gang beating people up. *Or* one that didn't respect girls. Some of the people in my class had boyfriends like that; I'd heard them talking. Seemed to me they let themselves be treated like dirt.

Rees wouldn't ever treat anyone that way. And I wouldn't *want* anyone who treated me that way. Just because I sometimes had secret dreams about – well! Heroes, I suppose. Rescuing me from burning buildings, and suchlike. A bit embarrassing, really! But that didn't mean I wanted some great macho hulk. I remembered how Rees had once carried Mum's shopping from the car for her, and how afterwards Mum had said she wished all boys had those sort of manners. "He's a real gentleman, isn't he?"

Craig had honked and hooted, and even I had made vomiting noises. I mean, *a real gentleman*. Pur-lease! All the same, I knew I ought to be grateful. I *was* grateful! And I would show him that I was.

I scrambled out of bed, crawling over Bundle, who likes to sleep in the middle of my duvet and resents being disturbed, and went in search of my mobile. After patting all over the dressing table and all along the windowsill I had to put my glasses on, which in the end I always do. I just don't seem to have the sort of eyes that are trainable. It's so frustrating! Craig doesn't have to wear glasses. It ought to be the other way round, cos after all it wouldn't matter so much for a boy.

THAT IS AN EXTREMELY SEXIST REMARK. I am sure boys are every bit as sensitive as girls about the way they look. Well, most boys. I am not actually sure about Craig. Sometimes I think he is about as sensitive as a block of cement. Anyway. The glasses were on my bedside table, and so, I discovered, was my mobile. I clambered back into bed with it and called Rees's number.

"'Lo?" His voice sounded sleepy.

I said, "Rees?"

"Polly?" I could see him struggling to sit up, his eyes still glued together.

"Sorry," I said, "did I wake you? What's the time?"

"Quar pars sen."

"Quarter past seven?" I shrieked it down the receiver. "God, is that all? I didn't realise! D'you want me to call back?"

"No, 's all right, I'm awake now. What's the emergency?"

"I just wanted to find out how you did last night."

"I got through to the finals." He said it modestly, cos unlike some people I could name, for example my brother, he is quite a modest sort of person. But I could tell he was pleased.

I cried, "Yay!" and bounced on the bed. Bundle made a grumbling noise and buried his nose in his tail by way of protest. *He* knew it was too early on a Sunday morning to be awake. "That is so clever," I said, admiringly. I asked him when the finals were, so that I could be sure to be there.

Rees said, "Well, but only if you really want to. I can see it might be a bit of a bore for anyone who doesn't play chess."

I took a deep breath. "Maybe I ought to learn," I said.

"Really? Would you really like to?"

The honest answer was no. Chess was one of those

42

things, like skiing and skydiving and higher mathematics, or even lower mathematics if it comes to it, that I just didn't feel I had anything in common with. I mean, I couldn't see myself hunched over a chessboard for hours on end any more than I could see myself hurtling down a ski slope or climbing a mountain. But Rees sounded so eager I knew it was one of those times when you have to pretend. I find you quite often have to do this when you are friends with someone and don't want to run the risk of disappointing them.

"You've always said you didn't think you'd be any good at it."

"Well—" I stifled a sigh. "I guess I could always give it a go."

"I'm sure you'd get hooked," said Rees. "It's one of those games you can really get lost in."

I said, "Mm."

"I'll come round next Saturday and bring my portable chess set, shall I?"

I said, "Mm. OK."

"We'll make a start."

"Right."

"It'll be fun!"

Like trying out new recipes. Doing things together. *Sharing*.

"I love all the little pieces," I said, trying to rouse some enthusiasm. "The little horse things...they're cute."

"They're called knights. And the ones that look like castles, they're called rooks."

"*Rooks?*"

"Yes."

"Why?"

"I don't know, they just are. But there is a special move you can make with them, called *castling.*"

My heart was already beginning to sink. You know how it is when you're just *sure* you're not cut out for something?

"I've got a book here," said Rees. "*Chess for Beginners*. I'll take it in to school tomorrow and give it to Craig."

Weakly I said, "Thank you."

"At least you'll be able to learn how all the pieces move. Then we can get started on a proper game."

I thought, *Whoopee!* And then I grew ashamed of myself and thought that I was not being fair. Rees was so excited, and so happy, and here was I being all negative and practically determined in advance to fail. I'd said that I would try to learn and I *would* try to learn. I assured Rees that by next Saturday I would have read at least the first chapter of his book.

"I'll know all about the rooks and the knights and the prawns, and everything."

Rees gave a honking guffaw at the other end of the line. It is very offputting the way boys start to honk when

44

they get to a certain age. Of course, I know they can't help it.

"What's funny?" I said.

"They're pawns," said Rees, "not prawns!"

"I think prawn's better," I said. "Pawn sounds rude, like when people look up porn on the internet."

"That's porn, spelt p.o.r.n."

"I know that! I'm just saying. Saying it *sounds* like it."

"Oh. OK! Sorry."

I grunted. *Honestly*. As if I didn't know the difference between pawn-with-a-w and porn-with-an-r!

"Actually, you can play chess on the internet," said Rees.

I felt like retorting that I'd rather download porn spelt p.o.r.n, but I didn't cos it would just have been silly. And he had apologised.

"So when d'you want to come over?" I said. "Afternoon or evening?"

"I can't in the afternoon," said Rees. "I've got to go into school and watch them play football. It's some important match and we're all supposed to be there."

I said, "Yuck." I was glad we didn't have to do that at my school. For one thing it would have meant watching Jessamy James, who is a bit like Keri and in every team going, so that would be *double* yuck.

"I don't really mind," said Rees. "It's only now and again. Shall I come by after tea?"

45

I said that after tea on Saturday would be good. Craig would be out by then, at least I hoped he would, him and Darcie, looking like an egg yolk, and we could be civilised. Somehow, when Craig is around it is all noise and confusion. Never a moment's peace.

"I'm really looking forward to this," said Rees. "It'll be great when you've learnt how to play...we can spend hours at it!"

I squeaked excitedly, to show that I was also looking forward to it. Which I was, in a way. I mean, I was glad I was doing something to make Rees happy. But I still couldn't imagine spending hours hunched over a chessboard!

On Monday after school Craig came home with the book Rees had promised me. He said, "*Chess for Beginners*? You gotta be joking!"

I said, "Do you mind?" and snatched the book from him. "Rees is going to teach me."

"Might as well try to teach Bundle," said Craig.

I glared at him. "What do you know about it?"

"I can play chess! But you won't be able to...it's not a girl's game."

I shrieked, "*Mu-u-um!* Did you hear that? You sexist PIG!"

Mum said, "I heard it. Craig, I believe it's your turn to take Bundle out. I suggest you go immediately, before it starts to rain."

Craig shouted, "I'm going! I'm not staying here to be insulted."

I said, "You insulted me first!"

"Just told it like it is," said Craig, "that's all."

The back door slammed behind him. "He is just *so* annoying," I grumbled.

"I think he's feeling a bit insecure," said Mum. "I'm not sure how well his date went the other day."

"Really?" My ears pricked up at once.

"Yes, but don't say anything, it's just a feeling I have; I may be wrong. And you can prove *him* wrong! I'm sure you'll pick up chess in no time."

I really worked at it. I had all my homework to do first, cos we have simply masses every single day, but when I went to bed I sat up for ages reading *Chess for Beginners, Chapter One*, all about the little pieces and the moves they could make.

Some were easy, even for me. Like the king can only move one square, in any direction, and the queen moves in straight lines in any direction, while the bishops move in diagonals and the pawns can only move *forward*, one square at a time, except for their first move, when they can move two squares. And then it said they could do something else, something about capturing other pawns "in passing", which however many times I read it still didn't make any sense and started to get me in a panic. I read it over and over, and

I still didn't know what it was talking about! How stupid could I be??? I went back to reread about the ones that looked like castles but could be called rooks, cos that hadn't made much sense, either. Rooks, it said, could move in rows and columns, only I didn't know what rows and columns were, and it didn't explain, so then I got in even more of a panic. I was too dumb even to understand simple basic moves! As for the cute little horsey ones, the knights, they moved in an L shape, but what was an L shape? Sort of...donk, donk! But in which direction? And how many squares? Lots at the same time, or just one? It didn't tell you! And this was *Chess for Beginners*...

I spent all night dreaming about chessboards, with knights madly leaping in L shapes and bishops zipping along on diagonals, with big bullyboy rooks tanking about in rows and columns, crushing all the poor little pawns underfoot. I told Mum despairingly next morning that I didn't think I'd ever get the hang of it.

"It's all so *complicated*."

"You could try asking Craig," said Mum. "He might be able to help you."

I said, "I'm not asking him!"

"Well, suppose we look at it tonight," said Mum. "Just you and me. See if we can't figure it out."

"Not if he's around," I muttered.

I had a whole *load* of homework that evening, and the

next, and by the time I'd struggled through it I really didn't feel like having to cudgel my brains all over again, trying to work out chess moves. In any case, Craig was there, and I wasn't going to let him know I couldn't even make sense of a book that was meant for beginners.

I asked Chloe during morning break on Wednesday whether she played chess, cos Chloe is one of those people; she has the sort of brain that is good at puzzles and stuff like those shape things, when you're shown lots of different shapes and have to say which ones would fit into other ones. I just can't ever see it, not even when it's been explained to me, but Chloe can. Anyway, she'd never played chess and didn't know anything about it so that wasn't any good.

I thought to myself that it wasn't fair, being expected to do all my homework and then start worrying about rows and columns and pawns jumping on other pawns. I mean, once you've written an essay for English, and an essay for history, and learnt a whole bunch of stuff for geography, not to mention French and science and the dreaded maths, you feel just about wiped out. So I decided I would devote the whole of Saturday afternoon to getting chess moves into my head. Maybe if I hadn't had to wear my brain to a frazzle beforehand I would be able to understand them a bit better. It would probably come to me in a blinding flash, as things sometimes do. *Oh,* I would think, *I've got it!* And then with any luck

I would still be able to remember it when Rees arrived. That was a far more sensible idea.

Unfortunately, things didn't work out quite the way I'd planned. It's funny how they never seem to; not with me, anyway. What happened was, Keri rang up to ask if I felt like going round her place again, Saturday afternoon. I immediately said yes – yes, yes! – forgetting all about *Chess for Beginners* and my vow to make some kind of sense of it before Rees turned up. I obviously must have sounded a bit surprised – I mean, it was only last Saturday we'd all been round there – cos Keri explained that Lily had suggested it. "I just had a text from her. I'll get back to her and say it's on. D'you want to call Frizz?"

As soon as I told Frizz that it had been Lily's idea, Frizz said, "Hah! Told you so."

"You think she's found someone?"

"Betcha," said Frizz.

We wondered whether she would come straight out and tell us, or whether we would have to worm it out of her. Knowing Lily, I thought we'd probably have to worm it out. But she obviously *wanted* us to know, or she wouldn't have suggested our getting together again so soon.

Frizz and I met up as usual. We got to Keri's place a few minutes early.

"Hi, guys!" Keri said.

I said, "Hi. Is Lily here yet?"

"Not yet, she's on her way. She sent me another text. Wanted to make sure you two were both coming!"

"We think she's got someone," said Frizz.

I said, "Yes! We think she's in love."

"God, you could be right!" cried Keri. "I bet it's that Joel person. Don't worry! I'll get it out of her."

She did, too. Me and Frizz would probably have tried to be a bit cunning, like leading up to it gradually, looking for clues. Keri couldn't be bothered with any of that. She gave us a few minutes of general chat then went bulldozing straight in.

"OK!" She leaned forward, subjecting Lily to a penetrating gaze. "You might as well come clean."

Lily turned a pretty shade of pink. She widened her eyes and said, "Come clean about what?"

"You know," said Keri. "C'mon!" She snapped her fingers. "Spill the beans! Who is it?"

Lily, very prim and proper, said, "I don't understand what you're talking about."

"Oh, please!" said Keri. "Don't give me that!"

So then Lily giggled and turned a bit pinker. But she wasn't embarrassed; she was loving it!

"It's Joel," said Keri, "isn't it?"

This time Lily went off into whole peals of giggles.

"Tell," said Keri. "Tell, tell!"

Me and Frizz took up the chant. "Tell, tell, tell!"

She had to, it was one of our rules: *no secrets*. But she

quite plainly wanted to. By now she was a deep ruby red. She admitted that it was Joel. He was in her ballet class, in her *pas de deux* class, and her dancing teacher had put him and Lily together because they made such a good team.

"You mean, you're partners," I said.

Lily nodded, ecstatically.

"Is he gorgeous?" said Frizz.

Lily rolled her eyes to say, like, you'd better believe it! We instantly bombarded her with questions. Was he tall? Was he dark? What was his surname? Lily said he was dark, not especially tall – "I'm too short to have a partner that's tall" – and that his surname was da Souza (which rang a sort of bell, though I couldn't immediately think why). "His dad is from Portugal."

It sounded so romantic! I said, "Joel da Souza…" And I went almost as pink as Lily as I said it. Goodness knows why. But it doesn't take much to make me blush.

Frizz, in tones of solemn rapture, said, "*The Sugar Plum* pas de deux *was danced to perfection by Lily Dugard and Joel da Souza.*"

Then I remembered: da Souza was one of the names Lily had been thinking of calling herself. Hmm…

Lily giggled again. She'd been in an almost continuous state of giggle ever since she'd got here. "It's not a *pas de deux*! It's just 'The Dance of the Sugar Plum Fairy'."

"And he obviously wouldn't dance that," said Keri.

"Not unless he was doing a drag number. Is he likely to do a drag number?"

Lily looked at her, puzzled. "You mean like the Ugly Sisters? In *Cinderella*? It's usually older dancers who do that."

"What I'm saying," said Keri, "what I'm trying to find out… Is he gay?"

Lily faltered. It was Frizz who boldly said, "Why should he be?"

"Well, you know…lots of male dancers are. I'm only *asking*," said Keri.

I really didn't see what business it was of hers. I mean… "What's wrong with being gay?" I said.

"There's nothing *wrong* with it. I'm not making judgements."

"So why would it matter?"

"Yes," said Lily. "Why would it matter?"

"Well, it wouldn't. Except—"

"What?" Lily demanded.

"She could still be in love with him," I said.

"Oh, God, you're so naive!" said Keri.

I was beginning to feel somewhat cross; Keri can get you like that. "I don't see why you can't be in love with someone just cos they're gay!"

"Well, you *can* be," said Keri, "if you want to be. I didn't say you couldn't. But it wouldn't be very sensible cos nothing could ever come of it."

I frowned. Lily was starting to look a bit bothered. Frizz, speaking very carefully, said, "I s'pose what it is… You couldn't actually have a *boyfriend* who was gay."

"Why not?" said Lily.

"Cos he wouldn't be a boyfriend…he'd just be a friend."

"And anyone who thinks otherwise," said Keri, "is obviously not ready for a mature relationship." Like she was such an expert? I'd have thought Frizz was the expert, if anyone was. She and Darren had been an item for ages, whereas Keri hopped like a flea from one boy to another. I didn't call *that* having mature relationships.

"Well, anyway," said Lily, in slightly sulky tones, "we're going to see the new *Swan Lake* this evening, the two of us, so there!"

"Just don't get up to anything I wouldn't," said Keri. "Not that there's much I wouldn't get up to!"

"*I'm* going to learn chess," I said. It wasn't as exciting as going to *Swan Lake* with a gorgeous boy called Joel da Souza, but it was better than nothing. "Rees is going to teach me."

"Ooh, boffin stuff!" said Keri.

Afterwards, as usual, we walked back down the hill together, me and Lily and Frizz.

"Have a good time," I called, as Lily ran off for her bus. Lily called back, "And you!"

"She's got it really bad," said Frizz, shaking her head.

"She's deep in love," I said.

"I just hope she doesn't get hurt."

I said, "Why should she? I don't see why she should!"

"If he's gay," said Frizz.

"*Oh*," I said, exasperated, "why is everyone so *prejudiced*?"

"I'm not prejudiced," said Frizz, "but Lily is so kind of…innocent. She's not streetwise like the rest of us. Not when it comes to boys."

I thought how once upon a time that would have sounded really funny, coming from Frizz. Just a few months ago she'd been the one that was innocent, always falling behind, always needing to have stuff explained. Now here she was, firmly putting herself in the same category as me and Keri: *streetwise*. I couldn't help feeling pleased, though, that she'd included me!

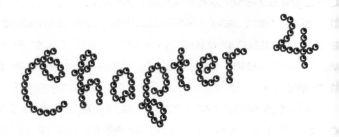

Chapter 4

I got home to find Craig on his way out with Bundle. I was, like, stupefied. (A really good word meaning *totally knocked out*, cos when did Craig ever take Bundle for a walk when it wasn't his turn???)

I asked him what he was doing and he said, "What's it look like I'm doing? I'm going up the park."

"But it's Saturday. You went yesterday!"

"So I'm being NICE!" roared Craig.

He bolted through the back door, slamming it behind him like he always does. I turned to Mum. "What's going on?"

"It was his idea," said Mum. "I think he's just trying to be helpful."

I said, "*Craig?*"

"Oh, come on," said Mum, "don't be ungracious!"

"He didn't have to shout," I muttered.

"No. Well…"

Well what? I sometimes think Mum makes excuses for Craig just because he's a boy and her favourite. Craig, on the other hand, says I am a daddy's girl and that I get away with stuff he would never be allowed to get away with. "Just because you're a girl!" he says. If this is true, it means that both Mum and Dad are incredibly sexist.

"To be honest," said Mum, "I think he just wanted to get out of the house. He's a bit upset at the moment. He was supposed to be going out with Debbie, or whatever her name is."

"Darcie," I said.

"Darcie; that's the one. Anyway, she's apparently going out with someone else. In other words, she's dumped him and he didn't even know about it until half an hour ago."

I said, "*Oh.*" I immediately felt mean that I'd complained about him shouting. I think it must be very terrible to be dumped. If Rees were to suddenly dump me I would probably go into a decline. It would just, like, *totally* destroy my confidence. Plus I would be convinced that everyone was going round whispering about me. "That's the girl Rees Nicholson dumped."

I reminded Mum that Darcie White was a truly horrible person. "She used to be a friend of Jessamy James."

Mum said, "Ah yes! The famous Jessamy."

Mum knows all about Jessamy. I used to come rushing home from primary school with tales of how unspeakably awful she was. I said that maybe I should try cheering Craig up by telling him he was better off *not* going out with anyone as horrid as Darcie, who in any case looked like an egg yolk, but Mum didn't seem to think that was such a good idea.

"Probably best not to mention it," she said. "Just.. you know! Humour him a little."

"You mean, like, make excuses," I said.

"I think maybe we should," agreed Mum. "Just this once."

You see? This is exactly what I mean! But on this occasion I didn't mind. I am not unreasonable! When Craig arrived back with Bundle I gave him a big THANK YOU. Craig said, "'S all right."

"I'll do it tomorrow," I promised.

He said, "Yeah. Whatever."

Mum beamed at me, and nodded. But then Dad came back from work and nearly blew it, being all loud and daddish, demanding to know who was going out on the razzle tonight, then?

"Craigie Baby? Poll Doll? All dressed up in our glad rags!"

I can't believe even Dad thought that jeans and T-shirts were glad rags. Craig's jeans had paint stains over them, *and* he hadn't gelled his hair. A sure sign he wasn't going anywhere. But Dad has no idea about fashion.

"So where is it tonight, then, eh?" He grinned at us

s he washed his hands at the sink. "Some rave omewhere?"

Craig scowled, and kept his head down. I said, "I'm taying in. Rees is coming over; he's going to teach me iow to play chess." Craig didn't even jeer.

When Rees arrived Mum said we should go into the itchen, where it was nice and cosy. She promised that iobody would disturb us; not even Craig. I said, "*Specially* not Craig."

"Don't worry," said Mum. "He's got a new computer ¡ame to keep him occupied."

I said, "Oh, well, if he's busy zapping things he'll be here all night. It's horrible," I grumbled to Rees, as we vent through to the kitchen. "All he wants to do is kill iliens. Why does everything have to be about killing? Vhy can't they have games where people meet and fall n love?"

"You could design one," said Rees.

"I could *write* one." I couldn't actually design one, as am not very good with computers. "Maybe I could do he story and you could turn it into a game?" I said, iopefully. I had this idea that, if he was keen, we could pend time making a game instead of playing chess, vhich I just *knew* wasn't going to work out.

But Rees said that computers weren't really his thing. Je said, "Craig could do it for you. He's a real boff!"

I said, "Huh!" Craig is like some kind of mad geek. He

practically *is* a computer. On the other hand, he couldn'
write a story to save his life! "He only likes games that ar
violent," I said. "Battles and stuff."

"Chess is like a battle," said Rees. "A battle of wits..
Let's get started! Have you managed to learn th
moves?"

I said that I had learnt most of them. "Only there wer
some bits I couldn't properly understand."

"Like what?" said Rees.

I thought when I told him that he would roll his eyes
Craig would have done! But like Frizz said, Rees is
really sweet person. Very patiently he explained to me a
about rows and columns, and showed me how th
horsey pieces, the knights, did their little prances roun
the board.

"See? It's easy! Now we'll try a practice game."

That was when it all started to go wrong. Practicall
from the beginning. It wasn't Rees's fault; it was mine
I just don't seem to have any powers of concentration!

Rees kept telling me how you have to look ahead
"You can't just think, *Oh, I'll move one of my pawns, o
I'll capture that bishop* – you have to think what's goin
to happen after you've done it. What the *consequence.
are going to be. Like, *If I do this, what will he do*? And,
he does that, what will I do? D'you see what I mean?"

I meekly said yes, and strained my eyes at the board
trying to be intellectual and think of consequences.

"Try to see it as a whole," said Rees. "Work out a strategy."

I said, "You mean, like, a plan?"

Rees said, "Yes! A plan."

Unfortunately I have never been much good at planning; I think I am quite a haphazard sort of person. Even when I write, it's all over the place, but at least with writing you can go back and tidy things up. You can't do that with chess.

"Take your time," said Rees. "There's no rush. *Concentrate.*"

I tried. I really did! I stared and stared at the board, mentally whizzing my bishops along their diagonals, having my knights leap over the other pieces and my rooks barrelling up and down their columns, but I obviously have a mind like a sort of popcorn machine. Stray thoughts kept shooting up out of nowhere, like, *I wonder how Lily is getting on with Joel?* and, *I wonder if they are holding hands?* and even, *What made Darcie dump Craig?*

It was such a mean thing to do! He might be a pain with *me*, cos of me being his sister, but he wouldn't have been a pain with her. Even with me, he isn't always; he can sometimes be quite reasonable. *Sometimes.* Not very often. But he still didn't deserve to be dumped! Especially after only one date.

All the time I was thinking these thoughts I dithered

about which of my pieces to move, and in the end I just chose blindly, in a panic, and Rees said, *"Why did you do that?"* and I didn't know the answer.

"Your rook!" He stared at me, like, unbelieving. "Why did you move your rook?" Helplessly I said that it seemed like a good thing to do.

"Well, it wasn't," said Rees, "cos now I'm going to move my bishop and in another couple of moves I'm going to checkmate you. See? That's what comes of not looking ahead!"

He sounded quite stern, so I felt like I was back in primary school, being told off for not paying attention. Or like I sometimes feel when Dad is trying to help me with my maths homework, and it doesn't matter how many times he explains things, I still can't grasp it. Dad finds it really exasperating! He can never understand how anyone can be that dumb.

Rees said, "OK, let's try again. I think you're starting to get the hang of it."

I knew he said it just to make me feel better. But I pretended to agree with him cos it seemed only fair.

Humbly I admitted that I shouldn't have moved my rook. "I can see that, now." I couldn't really. I still didn't understand how it was going to lead to checkmate. But Rees was trying *so* hard. "I'll be more careful next time."

"Just think ahead," urged Rees.

I was thinking ahead like mad when the door opened and Craig came bursting in. I said, "What are you doing in here?"

"Come for some milk," said Craig. He poured himself a glass and leaned against the sink, frowning across at the chessboard. My hand reached out, uncertainly, to move a pawn. Surely just moving one little unimportant piece like that couldn't bring disaster crashing round my ears? I heard Craig suck in his breath. Immediately I pulled my hand back and let it hover over a bishop, instead. Craig shook his head. "Don't wanna do that," he said.

I said, "Why not?"

"Leave yourself wide open."

"She's got to learn for herself," said Rees.

I said, "Yes, I don't need you butting in. You're not s'posed to be in here, anyway. Just take your milk and go!"

"Might want another glass," said Craig. He moved across to the table and stood there, making a great show of guzzling and slurping. "Good for you, milk is."

"Don't worry about him," said Rees. "You can move your bishop if you want."

I said, "No! Something bad will happen."

"Yes, but what? That's what you have to work out."

I sat there, gnawing on my lower lip. If we played this game much longer my lips would be, like, totally *shredded*.

"It's no use," said Craig. "You're wasting your time. You can't teach 'em! Their brains are wired differently."

He was only saying it to provoke me. Unfortunately, in my case, I knew it to be true. It was Rees who protested. He said, "I know girls that are really good."

"Probably lesbos," said Craig.

That was going *too* far. "Just get out!" I said. "Mum told us we could have the kitchen to ourselves!"

"All right, all right," said Craig. "I'm going. Don't have to get all bent out of shape. Don't have to SHOUT, either!"

He could talk. What cheek! He stuck his head back round the door. "You only want to be alone so you can get up to things."

I nearly shrieked, "What things?" but – thank goodness – I managed to stop myself just in time. Even as it was, I went into instant blushing mode.

"I don't know how you can bear to be friends with him," I muttered, as the door banged shut.

Rees said, "Craig's OK. He doesn't mean half of what he says. D'you want to carry on with this or would you rather do something else?"

A great wave of relief washed over me. "Let's do something else," I said.

"So what shall we do?"

For a minute I thought perhaps he might be hinting that we should *get up to things,* and I blushed even more furiously. But all he meant was, what should we do instead of playing chess.

"I don't get the feeling your heart's really in it," he said. He sounded almost apologetic, like it was his fault. "Maybe I should teach you bridge, instead."

I said, "*Bridge?*" I could feel my face scrunch up in horror. Hastily, I smoothed it out again. "Bridge is a card game," I said.

"Yeah! It's brilliant."

"But it's for *old* people."

"No, it's not! It's for anyone. It'd probably be more your thing than chess. I mean…some of the cards, they're really pretty."

I looked at him, rather hard. Now it was his turn to blush. "Sorry," he mumbled. "I didn't mean that. I was just trying to get you interested."

I took a breath, deep and quivering. "OK! I'll give it a go, if you really want…but I don't know much about card games!" I'd only ever played snap, and that was when I was young. Even then Craig was always yelling out ahead of me.

"Got to start somewhere," said Rees. He was all bright and eager. He really was trying. He obviously *wanted* us to do things together. "I'll tell you what," he said, "next Saturday…we could always go and watch the football."

I said, "*More* football?"

"Under Fifteens. Craig's playing."

65

"Oh, joy," I said.

"Yeah, well – you know! It's quite a big thing for him; he's been trying to get on the team for ages."

And he had just been dumped by his girlfriend. Resignedly, I said all right, I would go.

"He'd really appreciate it," said Rees.

I said, "Huh!"

"Then afterwards, we could go back to my place? That would give us the whole afternoon."

He sounded so happy about it. Why couldn't I be more enthusiastic? What was wrong with me? Didn't I *want* to learn things?

As I was seeing Rees off at the front door, Craig appeared, clumping down the stairs. "Ho ho ho," he said. "Who's been up to things?"

I withered him with a look – well, I tried to. Stupid little round faces like mine aren't really the right sort of shape for withering. You need a face like Keri's. Big, and bold, with bone structure.

Thinking of Keri, as I went to join Mum and Dad in front of the television, made me wonder: did she and her boyfriends *get up to things*? If so, what sort of things? Did they kiss and cuddle? Did they use *tongues*? I got quite hot and embarrassed just thinking about it. I tried to picture me and Rees kissing and cuddling and using tongues, and that made me even more hot and embarrassed. So much so that Mum looked at me in surprise and said, "You seem rather flustered! Are you all right?"

"She's been up to things," said Craig.

I roared, "I have not! I've been playing chess."

I really didn't know why I'd ever bothered feeling sorry for that boy. And to think I'd agreed to go and watch him play football!!! I decided that I must have been mad.

Chapter 5

On Sunday morning I couldn't resist the temptation to text Lily and find out how her date had gone. I wouldn't have texted Keri, cos she was out with someone different practically every week. I couldn't keep up with all the boyfriends Keri had had. They were all called by these posh names, like Justin, or Perry, or Damian, and they all sounded exactly the same. Like a load of clones; you sort of lost interest after a bit. But this was Lily's first real date and I was eager to hear what had happened. Well, actually, I suppose, what I really wanted to know was whether she'd kissed and cuddled. I didn't think she would have used the tongue; not first time round. But I couldn't help being curious!

Needless to say, she didn't tell me; not even so much as a hint. She just texted back *Date supa!* – which left me none the wiser. "Supa" wasn't even a Lily sort of word; it was a Keri word. I tried to read between the lines. Did that mean things hadn't gone well, so she was using a Keri-type expression to cover up? Or did it mean things had gone *so* well that only a Keri-type expression would do? I couldn't make up my mind.

It bugged me all day. I had to call Frizz, in the end, to ask her what she made of it. "What d'you think it means?"

"Who knows?" said Frizz. "I 'spect she'll tell us next time we meet."

"But that could be weeks away!"

"Well, ring her," said Frizz, "and ask."

I did try, but Lily didn't answer, and after that I got cold feet cos it seemed a bit too much like prying. I wasn't sure why I was so desperate to find out. I mean, what was it to me? Joel was Lily's boyfriend, not mine. Even if things hadn't worked out, he still wouldn't be interested in me. He was obviously gorgeous and I am just plain ordinary, so what was I getting so agitated about? It was something to do with his name...*Joel da Souza*. Plus the fact that he was a dancer. It was just so romantic! The sort of thing you could lie in bed and dream about. You couldn't really dream about going to a football match or learning how to play bridge. Definitely *not* romantic.

But I'd promised Rees I'd go with him, so Saturday morning I set off in the car with Dad and Craig. Dad was giving Craig a lift to school but couldn't actually stay to watch the match. He said, "Sorry, mate! I'd love to, but I'm way behind with a job. At least Polly'll be there, to cheer you on."

Craig looked about as excited at the prospect as I was. "I don't want you showing me up," he said.

How could I show him up? What did he think I was going to do? Start yelling and clapping and shouting his name?

"I'm only going to keep Rees company," I said.

"Well, don't show your ignorance."

Some nerve! But I have to admit, I don't actually understand football all that well. Last term Jessamy had got up a petition asking that we play football instead of netball, which she said was soft and soppy, but fortunately it was turned down. I am not a very sporty sort of person (another reason Joel da Souza probably wouldn't be interested in me), and the thought of being forced to run up and down a soggy playing field with Jessamy in hot pursuit, kicking and barging and accidentally-on-purpose grinding people into the mud – well! It was like my idea of a nightmare.

It was quite like a nightmare just having to stand and watch. I kept reminding myself that I was there to support Craig, who had been hurt and humiliated by Darcie White. Towards the end I got really cold and started shivering, so Rees took off his jacket and put it round my shoulders. I huddled inside it feeling all warm and cosy, wondering if maybe he would put his arm round me as well, but he didn't. If he had, I wouldn't have minded. I would have quite liked it. But there were lots of boys from his class standing around, so I expect probably it would have embarrassed him. I did hunch up to him as close as I could.

"Aren't you freezing?" I said.

Rees said, "No, I'm all right. There's only a few minutes to go."

I rubbed the tip of my nose, which was like a blob of ice. "I think football is such a boring game," I said.

"It's boring to play," agreed Rees.

"I think it's boring to watch."

"Well…yeah. I guess there are things I'd rather be doing. But you have to show an interest or they think there's something wrong with you."

"God, why is everyone so prejudiced?" I cried. "It's like Lily has this boyfriend that's a dancer, and Keri immediately thinks he's got to be gay. I mean, how prejudiced is *that*? And even if he was, what would it matter? They could still be friends!"

"Sure," said Rees.

"Well, they could!"

"Absolutely."

"I don't see why everyone gets so fussed. What difference does it make?"

"Well, it would make a *difference*," said Rees.

At that moment, someone scored a goal and a load of cheering broke out. Rees cheered, too; I guess he felt he had to.

"Anyway," I said, when things had quietened down, "she's probably got it wrong."

Rees said, "Who has?"

"Keri. About Lily's boyfriend...just because he's a dancer."

"Oh. Yeah! Maybe. We could go, now, if you like."

We went back on the bus to Rees's place, where his mum had some lunch waiting for us. "Hot soup," she said. "Get it down you, Polly, you look pinched." And then, turning reproachfully to Rees, "Fancy keeping her out there in this weather!"

"She had to stay," said Rees. "Craig was playing."

"Well, in that case I think it was very noble of you, Polly."

"It was," I said. "And I didn't do it for Craig; I did it cos *he* said I had to." I gave Rees a little push.

"You shouldn't let him bully you," said his mum. "What are you doing this afternoon?"

"I'm teaching her to play bridge," said Rees.

His mum raised an eyebrow. "Does she want to know how to play bridge?"

"Well, she couldn't get into chess, so—"

"So now you're inflicting bridge on her!"

"I'm not *inflicting*."

72

"Yes, you are! Polly, you must stand up for yourself. Do you really and truly want to learn bridge?"

I said, "Well…"

"Be honest!"

"I guess I could always try," I said.

I obviously didn't sound too convincing, cos the minute we were on our own, Rees said, "You don't really want to, do you?"

I heaved this big sigh.

"You don't have to," he said. "I was just trying to think of something we could…you know! Do. What would *you* like to do?"

My first vengeful thought was that I should make him come and watch Jessamy playing hockey, to pay him back for the football. But that would be like a cutting-off-my-nose-to-spite-my-face kind of thing. I'd be just as bored as he was. I might even be *more* bored.

"It's not really fair," said Rees, "if we only do things I like."

No, it wasn't! It was what I'd been thinking myself. But there wasn't much point being resentful when I couldn't make any suggestions of my own, such as, for example… what??? All I liked to do was write stories and poems and sit around gossiping. Well, I also liked trying out different hairstyles, and different kinds of makeup, and reading every teen magazine I could lay my hands on, especially the fashion articles and the problem pages and the latest hot news about my favourite celebs. God, I was such a shallow sort of person!

"Tell me what you'd usually be doing on a Saturday," said Rees.

I said, "Well…I s'pose I'd probably be mooching round the shopping centre." Shallow, shallow, *shallow*.

"By yourself?" said Rees.

"No, with Frizz." We hadn't done it for ages. Mostly, these days, she was off somewhere with Darren.

"So d'you want to do it with me?" said Rees.

I looked at him doubtfully. "Wouldn't it bore you?"

"Dunno," said Rees. "Never done it. But I'll give it a go! How about we meet there next Saturday?"

"All right," I said. Why not?

"Shopping?" said Chloe. She sounded well impressed! It was Monday morning, first break. We were strolling round the field together. Chloe had wanted to know what I'd done at the weekend, so I'd told her about being forced to stand for hours in the freezing cold watching football. Chloe had groaned and said, "Honestly! The *demands* they make." So then, feeling that I had to be fair to Rees, I'd told her how he'd suggested that on Saturday we did something which was my choice.

"I chose going round the shops!"

"And he's OK with it?"

"He says he wants us to do something we both enjoy. Not that he 'specially enjoys watching football, it's just that if he doesn't take an interest they'll think there's something peculiar about him. People are so prejudiced!" Before I could stop myself it all came bursting out yet again. Lily having a boyfriend who was a dancer, and Keri saying he had to be gay, and me saying what if he was? "I mean, really! What does it matter? What difference would it make?"

Chloe gave me this funny look, like *you have to be joking*. I at once wished I hadn't mentioned it. I didn't know why I had! It was getting to be like some kind of obsession.

"Anyway," I said hurriedly, "we're meeting in the shopping centre, Saturday afternoon. Not really to go *shopping*." You can't shop without money, and I was broke. "Just to mooch about."

Chloe said, "This is, like, totally extraordinary!"

I was puzzled. "How d'you mean?"

"Having a boyfriend who'll go round the shops with you! Men don't like shopping," said Chloe. "It's a known fact."

It was true that Dad didn't; he always said that being dragged on a shopping trip with Mum was worse than going to the dentist. And Craig only ever went to the shopping centre to play games in the arcade. Stricken, I said, "Maybe he'll hate it!"

"At least he's willing to give it a go," said Chloe.

I said, "Yes, I know. I ought to be grateful."

"So why aren't you?"

"I am, I am!"

"He just wants to make you happy. Most boys don't care. Well, they *do*," said Chloe, "but only if you'll do the sort of things they want to do. *Boy* things. Rees is obviously in touch with his feminine side."

Doubtfully I said, "Is that good?"

"Unless you're one of those little itsy-bitsy types that just wants some mindless macho hunk."

Hastily I said that I didn't want that. I wasn't an itsy-bitsy type!

"So what's your problem?" said Chloe.

"I don't have a problem!"

"So why d'you sound kind of, like, *but*?"

I said, "But?"

"Like, I know I'm lucky to have a boyfriend like that, *but*."

Chloe is very sharp; she picks up on the least little thing. Reluctantly, not wanting to be disloyal, I said I knew I was lucky and there wasn't really any but—

"*But?*"

"It's not romantic!" I wailed. Watching football, and playing chess, and going round the shops... "It's just *ordinary*!"

Chloe said, "I s'pose." And then, linking her arm

chummily through mine, she said, "D'you ever have daydreams?"

"Mm…sometimes," I said. I said it rather guardedly, because, I mean, it mightn't be normal. Did everyone have daydreams, or was it just me? If it was just me, then I wasn't sure I wanted to admit it.

"What sort of thing do you daydream about?"

"Well…" I was nervous of going into too much detail in case she laughed at me. Or in case it wasn't normal.

"You can tell me," said Chloe, squeezing my arm. "You tell me yours, then I'll tell you mine!"

"You have daydreams?" I said. I wanted to make certain.

Chloe said, "Everybody does!"

Yes, I thought, *but mine were really complicated ones*. More like stories. More like *books*. They went on for ever! I lay in bed at night and daydreamed myself to sleep. Then I woke up in the morning and daydreamed some more. I even dreamed on my way to school. Sometimes I even dreamed *in* school. And always about the same thing. This incredibly gorgeous, romantic boy that everybody fancied, only he fancied me – *me!* – and everybody was mad jealous. But him and me (he had lots of different names. Just now he was called Joel da Souza), we were an item. Hand in hand, we wandered through my daydreams; even, sometimes, locked in each other's

77

embrace with our lips pressed together, though not the tongue thing, we hadn't done that yet, mainly because I couldn't quite imagine what it would feel like. But anyway, towards the end of the dream something would happen, some kind of disaster, so that I would be in mortal peril and my gorgeous handsome boyfriend would come riding to my rescue—

"*Riding?*" said Chloe.

I came to, with a start. It was like she was breaking into my actual thoughts. I blushed, wondering how much I had said out loud.

"Riding on a horse?"

I blushed even more at that. I had, just occasionally, pictured him riding on a horse. Either a milk white steed or a jet black stallion, depending on my mood.

"Doesn't have to be a horse," I muttered. "Could be a bike. Could be anything! Point is, he rescues me."

"What from?"

"Whatever it is! Like I might be caught in a burning building and can't get out, or fell into an icy pond, or – I dunno! Be trapped in a bog."

Chloe giggled. "You mean, trapped in a loo?"

"Not a loo! A *bog*. Like you get sucked into."

"What, and he pulls you out?"

"Yes, but not just like that. There has to be a bit of a story to it."

"He probably tears a branch off a tree," said Chloe.

"That's what people do. And then he crawls along it and hauls you out."

Chloe has absolutely *no* idea how to build up a story. She is a very brainy person, far more of a boffin than I am, but she is no good at all at creative work.

"He doesn't actually manage to get me out until the very last minute," I said. "He's almost there when something happens, like the branch starts sinking and he's getting sucked in, so it's, like, really tense? And then in the nick of time, just as I'm about to disappear and die a horrible gurgling death, *that's* when he drags me out." *Straight into his arms*...only I didn't add that bit. I reckoned I'd said more than enough already.

Chloe was gazing at me like I was some curious form of prehistoric life. Rather crossly I said, "Well? What's yours?"

"Mine?" Chloe gave one of her happy cackles of laughter.

"You said you'd tell me yours if I told you mine!"

"Nothing to tell."

"You mean, you lied to me!" She'd just been having me on. And she was supposed to be my *friend.*

Chloe said, "I didn't lie. It's just that I don't make up stories like you...and if I did, I wouldn't be the one being rescued, I'd be the one doing the rescuing!"

I said, "*You?*" in these really scornful tones, cos to be honest I was a bit angry with her. She'd cheated me!

79

"Dunno how you think you could rescue anyone. *Spiderwoman!*" Chloe is a tiny little matchstick creature.

She tossed her head defiantly. "I'm a feminist," she said. "I don't dream about being rescued by *men*. Any case, it's not as odd as dreaming about being sucked into bogs!"

I said, "*Nearly* sucked. And I don't dream about that bit so much as the bit where he pulls me out." That was the really good part; the part that I mainly dwelt on. "Only thing is," I said, glumly, "it's always someone else." Some made-up person. Someone from my fevered imagination. "It's never Rees." I'd never dreamt about Rees. *Ever.*

"Well, give him a chance," said Chloe. She cackled again. "Maybe a raving maniac will attack you in the shopping centre and he can rush in and save you... Wham! Bam! Pow!" She spun in a circle, flailing her fists and throwing her legs in the air.

"He doesn't *do* kick boxing," I said.

"Holy crabcakes!" Chloe stopped spinning, and thrust her face close to mine. "Know what?" she said. "You're impossible!"

I wondered if it could be true. It is good to aim high, but maybe it is not always quite realistic. Like, for instance, if you happened to be tone deaf, which I am sometimes accused of being – "Cut out the dreadful noise!" people cry, stuffing their fingers in their ears the minute I start to sing. Well, in such a case it wouldn't be very realistic to have an ambition to be a pop star. Not really. Not unless a miracle were to occur.

But miracles *do* occur! I *could* meet a gorgeous romantic boy who fancied me. I could meet a gorgeous romantic boy who was blind, for instance. There isn't any reason a person who's blind can't be gorgeous and romantic. In some ways it might even make him *more* romantic. At any rate, he wouldn't want to stand around at football matches, *and* he wouldn't care that I have this silly little round babyish sort of face. He would fall in love with the inner me! And everybody, including Jessamy James, would be crazed with jealousy.

Well, I mean, you never know. Stranger things have happened.

In the meantime, I was going to mooch round the shops with Rees. When I told Frizz, she said, "Oh, that is so sweet of him!" Maybe it was; but it wasn't *romantic*. I couldn't see Joel da Souza going round the shops. Come to that, I couldn't really see Joel da Souza doing anything except dance. My imagination didn't stretch that far. What *did* gorgeous romantic people do? I hadn't the faintest idea!

Saturday afternoon, as I was about to set off for town, Craig appeared. "There's a word for people like you," he said.

I stared at him haughtily. "What word?"

"I dunno, I can't remember it, but I know there is one. Means you take men's masculinity away from them."

Coldly, I said, "What on earth are you on about?"

"Dragging poor old Knickers round the shops!"

"I am not dragging him," I said, "he *offered*. And don't call him that!" Just because his surname was Nicholson.

"Call him what I want," said Craig. "Call him Underpants, if I want."

"God, you're so childish," I said. "I'm not surprised Darcie dumped you!"

I knew it was mean, but I'd asked him *so many times* not to call Rees by that ridiculous name, and he still went on doing it. He did look a bit downcast, though. He muttered, "Darcie didn't dump me, I dumped her."

"Well, whatever," I said.

"It's true!"

"OK," I said. "All right!"

"Just so's you know."

I said, "Yes, well, just so's you know...*stop calling Rees Knickers!*"

I told Rees, when we met in the shopping centre, that Craig had accused me of dragging him there.

"You're not dragging me," said Rees. "I volunteered. What are we actually after, anyway? What are you going to buy?"

"I'm not here to *buy* things," I said. Not unless he had

any money, cos I certainly hadn't. Rees looked puzzled. "So what are we here for?"

"Just to...you know! Wander round."

Check out the latest fashions, try all the testers at the cosmetics counter, collect free samples, spray ourselves with perfume. That was what me and Frizz did. Rees seemed a bit bemused. He said, "Yeah, OK. Whatever!"

It didn't work. It wasn't Rees's fault; he was, like, totally patient. He didn't groan or sigh or make sexist remarks. But he just didn't get it, and after a bit I started feeling guilty, thinking that maybe I *was* the sort of person that took men's masculinity away from them – though to be honest I couldn't really see that going round the shops was any worse for a boy than being forced to watch football in the freezing cold if you were a girl.

Still, I did feel a bit sorry for Rees. He didn't come to life until we hit the top floor and he caught sight of a model shop, which I'd never even noticed before. They had a toy train going round and round on a big table, with lots of boys and men watching it. Just watching. Rees said, "Hey, look! A train!" and pulled me with him into the shop. Next thing I know, we've edged our way to the front and we're part of the crowd, watching. Just watching. The train wasn't even doing anything, apart from going round. It wasn't like it was crashing into other trains, or going off the rails, or sliding down embankments. Nothing exciting. Just going round.

After a bit I managed to wriggle my way free and went outside to sit on the edge of a big tub full of flowers. I wondered if Joel da Souza would be fascinated by the sight of a train going round. I felt sure that he wouldn't. Nor, of course, would the gorgeous romantic blind boy who I was going to meet. Where would I meet him? Maybe he would move into one of the houses in our road and I would bump into him on the way to school. No! *He* would bump into *me*. And I would say sorry, cos I always say sorry whether it's my fault or not, though come to think of it, it probably would be my fault if he was blind. So *I* would say sorry, then *he* would say sorry, then...

I sat happily on the edge of my flower tub, making up a new daydream. I'd almost forgotten about Rees; I was quite surprised when he suddenly appeared.

"Oh! There you are," I said.

Grinning a bit foolishly, he said, "I didn't realise you'd gone... Look, I bought you something."

He held out a tiny little model of..."What is it?" I asked.

"It's the London Eye! See, it goes round."

"Gosh," I said, "we could stand and watch it!" And then I remembered my manners and said thank you very much and that I would put it on my bedroom shelf along with all my china animals. Which I did, and it is still there to this very day! It was the first thing Rees had ever bought me. I knew he'd only done it because of feeling bad about not realising I had gone, but I was touched, all the same. I wondered if he would like me to kiss him for it. I thought he probably might; I thought I probably should. But I wasn't quite brave enough. Oh, when would I ever be???

Chapter 6

That night, when I went to bed, I started a new daydream about bumping into the incredibly handsome gorgeous blind boy. It was just starting to get really good when I fell asleep, which was most annoying. I woke up again at seven o'clock and tensed myself, waiting for Mum to yell at me like she always did: "Polly, if you don't get up you'll be late for school!" Then I remembered that it was Sunday, and there wasn't any school. More importantly, I didn't have to get up! I immediately dived back under the duvet to carry on with my daydream, only for some reason I couldn't seem to get things going again. There was something wrong! It wasn't working.

Maybe it was cos I'd told Chloe and she'd laughed at me, so now I was feeling self-conscious. But it was *my* daydream, not hers! I could daydream about anything I liked.

It still wasn't working. And suddenly I realised: how

could someone who was blind, no matter how gorgeous, come to my rescue? He couldn't! It was far more likely I'd have to go to his. Well, that was all right, I could do that. I was just as feminist as Chloe!

The trouble is, I am not a very brave sort of person. Confronted by danger, I would probably fly into an instant panic and start screaming. Even just dreaming about it was enough to bring me out in goose bumps. I was quite glad when Mum called upstairs that I'd better get myself out of bed if I wanted any breakfast.

I was surprised, that afternoon, to have a telephone call from Lily. Rather breathlessly, she gabbled, "We're having a demo day next Saturday and me and Joel are doing a *pas de deux*. I don't s'pose you and Rees would like to come?"

I said, "We'd love to! What's a demo day?"

Lily said it was like a sort of showcase. People from different classes were chosen to demonstrate what they had achieved during the past twelve months.

"We had one last year and Keri came, but I'm not asking her this time. Not after what she said about Joel. She might make some sort of remark – you know what she's like."

"Tactless," I said.

"This is it," said Lily. "She's *tactless*. So I thought maybe you and Rees would like to come? Cos you're not the sort of people to be prejudiced or make remarks. And it only lasts a couple of hours; it'll all be over by nine o'clock. My mum said she'd take us out for a meal afterwards and drop everybody home. Unless, of course—" a note of doubt crept into Lily's voice. She suddenly sounded a bit unsure of herself. "Unless you've arranged something else?"

Fortunately, we hadn't. We were going to go for a walk on Sunday, with the dogs – that is, my dog, Bundle, and Rees's dog, Rufus – but we hadn't made any plans for Saturday. Even if we had, I'd have cancelled them like a shot! I felt incredibly flattered to be asked. I mean, me instead of Keri! But Keri was tactless: I could be trusted. We both could; Rees as well as me.

"I always think that Rees is *civilised*," said Lily.

"Unlike my brother," I said. "If you'd asked me to bring *him* – well, I just wouldn't, that's all!"

"This is what I feel about Keri. I don't want to be *embarrassed*," said Lily.

I promised that I would not embarrass her, and she said, "I know you won't. That's why I asked you."

I was quite proud to be able to tell Rees that we had been invited to Lily's demo day. "Cos we're civilised," I said. "And not prejudiced."

"Prejudiced about what?" said Rees.

"Oh! Boys doing ballet. That sort of thing. You're not prejudiced," I said, "are you?"

"I try not to be," said Rees.

"But even if you were, you wouldn't make remarks?"

"Of course I wouldn't!" He said it indignantly, like, *how could you think such a thing?*

"It's all right," I said, "I'm just checking. Cos Lily doesn't want to be embarrassed."

"Why should I embarrass her?"

"Well, you wouldn't," I said. "That's why she's asked us."

Rees shook his head, like it was all beyond him.

"Don't worry," I said. "It'll be fun!" I nearly added, *far more fun than football*...

Craig, needless to say, couldn't resist a bit of silly macho jeering, but wonder of wonders! Mum put him in his place. "We'll have none of that sort of talk," she said. "It's not clever, it's just rather stupid." Craig went red and slunk out of the room, so that for a moment I almost felt sorry for him. He's not used to Mum telling him off. He did deserve it, though!

Keri rang on Friday. "I hear you're going to Lily's demo day," she said. I thought perhaps she was going to be resentful, being Lily's best friend and all, but to my relief she sounded quite cheerful. "Just as well she didn't ask me – I'd never get Damian going to watch boys poncing about in tights!"

I'd never met the great Damian Whitchurch, but I guessed he was probably another of the big beefy macho types she fancied. As far as I was concerned, she could keep them!

"Anyway, this is just to remind you," said Keri, "I want a full report on you-know-who!"

In all my life, I'd never been to a display of ballet before. I wasn't quite sure what to expect. I just hoped it wouldn't be all pink and soft and frilly. Well, I suppose, really, I hoped that Joel wouldn't be pink and soft and frilly. And oh, bliss, he wasn't! He was everything I'd dreamt of. Dark-skinned and drop-dead gorgeous! Black hair, very thick and glossy. Deep brown eyes, flashing white teeth…cliché, cliché, cliché! (As Mrs Pollard, my English teacher, would say.) But I can't help it – I can't think of any other way to describe him! Butterflies flitted in my stomach all the time he was on stage.

He and Lily did this number together. Joel was wearing a white singlet and scarlet tights, while Lily had a scarlet top and one of those very short, stiff, sticky-out skirts that dancers wear. A tutu! That was it. I remembered Lily being really excited when she got to wear one for the first time. I tried my hardest to watch her as much as I watched Joel, cos she was doing all this truly clever and amazing stuff with her legs, not to mention whizzing about all over the place on the tips of her toes, but mostly my eyes were glued to Joel. I felt quite guilty when Rees whispered in my ear. "Lily's really good, isn't she?"

I'd hardly noticed her! But I couldn't help whispering back, "So is Joel!"

Rees agreed that he was: "They both are." I hoped he wasn't just saying it to humour me.

That night in bed I daydreamed about Joel. He was so gorgeous! I did so *so* envy Lily. I wished so much that I could be like her, tiny and pretty and dainty, instead of a short dumpy kind of person with a face like a squidgy bun. Someone like Joel wouldn't look twice at me! Except in my daydreams…anything can happen in daydreams. That's what is so wonderful about them! It doesn't matter how soppy they are. It doesn't matter if they are just, like, *totally* unrealistic. I mean, daydreams are harmless, right? Nobody expects them to come true. I knew that Joel was Lily's boyfriend, not mine. I knew that he wasn't ever going to rescue me from a burning building, or a bog, or from anything else; and even if he did, we wouldn't end up in each other's arms. I knew all that! But I could still daydream.

As a matter of fact, although I had absolutely no idea at the time, part of my daydream *was* about to become true. Not the part about Joel; the other part. The part where I am in mortal peril and have to be rescued…

I woke on Sunday morning without the least suspicion of what was to befall me. Just as well, cos I am *such* a coward. Rees and I had agreed that we were going to go on a long, long walk, right across the Downs, starting off from the car park, which is at the end of Rees's road, then right along the ridge to the far end, down the hill and into the valley, and all the way through the woods back to the car park.

"We'll be at least two hours," I told Dad, as he dropped me and Bundle off.

"Well, give us a call when you want to be picked up," said Dad.

Craig, who for some reason had insisted on accompanying us, opened the passenger door and started to get out.

"What are you doing?" I said.

"Thought maybe I ought to go with you. Keep an eye on things."

I said, "What things?"

"*Thing*s," said Craig. "Like, you know…things!" And he scrunched up his face and squeezed one eye tight shut. "I feel I ought to be there to look after you."

"I'm sure that if she needs any looking after, Rees can manage perfectly well," said Dad.

"And anyway," I said, "why should I need looking after? I'm not a child!"

"Actually, you are," said Craig.

"Well, so are you," I said, "if it comes to that, so I don't know what use you think you'd be!"

"A lot more use than Knickers."

I felt my face growing crimson with rage. He was doing it again! How many times did I have to ask him?

I opened my mouth to protest, but he simply talked right across me. "Imagine if you slipped and went over the edge of the quarry... I could abseil down and get you. He couldn't! He wouldn't know how."

"She's not going to go over the edge of any quarries," said Dad. "She's going to stay well away. So is Bundle. Right?"

I said, "Right!"

"I'm just saying," said Craig. "I ought to go with them."

Simply because he couldn't think of anything better to do, that's all it was.

"Dad, I don't want him!" I wailed.

"Then you don't have to have him," said Dad. He is a whole lot firmer with Craig than Mum is. "You," he said to him, "back in the car! Polly, enjoy your walk, and I'll see you later."

I didn't fall over the edge of the quarry cos I made sure not to go anywhere near it. I wouldn't have done, anyway. I might *daydream* about being in mortal peril and having to be rescued, but I didn't necessarily want it to happen in real life. If I'd known it was going to, I'd never have got out of the car.

How it happened was, we were walking along a path down in the valley, with the dogs off hunting and me and Rees just happily ambling, side by side, when my mobile rang. It was Keri, impatient to hear about Joel, so I sank down at the base of a tree to be comfortable and have a chat. Rees sat down next to me. He had that resigned look that boys sometimes have when girls get gossiping on the phone. (Like boys can't gossip, too! I've heard Craig going at it.)

"So tell, tell!" said Keri. "Did you meet him? What's he like?"

I said, "To die for!"

"Super bliss?"

"Super bliss!"

"Out of ten? Eight, nine? Nine and a half?"

"More like eleven!"

Keri squealed. We both squealed.

"You're not joking me?"

"No! You ought to see him!"

"She won't let me," said Keri. She gave a loud guffaw down the telephone. "Terrified I might pinch him!"

"I think, actually, she's just scared you'd embarrass her," I said.

"Me? How would I embarrass her?"

"Saying he might be gay."

"*Is* he?"

"No!"

"I bet he is! Let's face it," said Keri, "you wouldn't know."

I said, "I would, too!"

"*I* would," said Keri.

"I was there," I said.

"Yes, but you're so naive. So's Lily…you both are."

I breathed, very heavily, like a grampus. Whatever a grampus was. Obviously some kind of heavy-breathing creature. Rees looked at me and raised an eyebrow. I pulled a face.

"You're like a couple of big babies," said Keri. "You are just *so* naive! You haven't a clue when it comes to boys!"

"Honestly," I grumbled, as we rang off, "Keri is such a know-all."

"She's right, though," said Rees. "He probably is gay."

I glared at him accusingly. "How can you say that? You hardly even spoke to him!" We'd only met him for a few minutes, after the show. I'd been too tongue-tied to say anything at all, and Rees had mainly talked to Lily. So what did he know?

"I only said *probably*," said Rees.

I told him, crossly, that he was as bad as Keri. "Always thinking you know everything!" But I didn't want us to quarrel, so as I stuffed my phone back in my pocket, I said, "What d'you think a grampus is?"

"I know what it is," said Rees. "I know everything! It's another name for a whale. Now apologise!"

I never got the chance, because at that moment the world suddenly erupted into a fury of buzzing and hissing. Bundle, who had been investigating a hole at the base of the tree, gave a sudden terrified yelp and shot off with his tail between his legs, shaking his head frantically from side to side. Rees cried, "We're sitting on a wasps' nest!" and jumped to his feet, pulling me after him.

We ran as fast as ever we could, but no way could we outrun a swarm of angry wasps. They buzzed all about us in a great cloud, burying themselves in our hair and clinging to our clothes. I would like to be able to report that I remained cool and calm in the face of danger, but in fact I flew into an immediate panic and started screaming and swatting and flapping with my arms. In the end, when they finally gave up, it was Rees who told me to stand still while he picked every last wasp off me – *before he picked them off himself.* He then picked them off Bundle and Rufus, who had also panicked, though nowhere near as badly as me.

I felt so ashamed of myself that when I discovered I'd been stung I did my best not to make a fuss about it, since after all it was only a tiny little sting and it was only on my arm.

"It's all right," I said, determined to be brave. "It doesn't really hurt that much."

"Spit on it," said Rees.

I spat, vigorously, and rubbed. "At least it's better than a bee sting," I said. "Bee stings stay in you. W-w-wasps-s-s—" My voice faded out. I stood, swaying.

"Polly? What's the matter?" said Rees. "What's wrong?"

I didn't know what was wrong; I was suddenly feeling most peculiar. Sick, and dizzy, and almost like I might faint. My tongue seemed to be swelling up, and my throat, so that I couldn't breathe properly. I heard Rees saying, "Polly! Talk to me!" and then I found myself slowly crumpling up, lying on the ground, with Rees on his knees beside me. He seemed to be kissing me, but that couldn't be right. What would he be kissing me for? He kept saying, "Polly! Polly!" but my throat had closed up and I couldn't talk. I couldn't swallow, I couldn't breathe. I was dimly aware of Bundle, licking my face and whimpering, then everything faded to blackness.

The next thing I knew, I was waking up in hospital…

Chapter 7

"A wasp sting?" said Keri. "You nearly died from a *wasp* sting?"

"You can," said Frizz, "if you get stung in the mouth. It makes you all swell up so you can't breathe."

"Yow!" Lily clutched dramatically at her throat.

"Did you get stung in the mouth?" said Keri.

I said, "No, I got stung on the arm, but I still swelled right up."

"I never heard of anyone doing that! I've been stung loads of times," boasted Keri.

"Yes," I said, "but you're not allergic. I have this special condition called...something or other. Anna something...makes you go into shock."

They all three fell silent, staring at me in a sort of awe. A fortnight had passed since I'd woken up in hospital, and we were at Keri's, the four of us, sitting around on big puffy floor cushions.

"Anaphylactic," I said proudly.

"Come again?" said Keri.

I spelt it out for them: "Anna-fill-act-ic." I'd had a bit of trouble with it myself, just at first, but I'd wanted to learn so I could tell people. I mean, it is quite interesting. "It's an *allergic reaction*," I said. "It only happens if you're over-sensitive."

Frizz was looking worried. "But how would you know?"

I told her that you wouldn't. "Not till it happened."

"Could always go and poke a wasps' nest," said Lily. She gave a happy chortle. "Then you'd find out quick enough!"

Both Frizz and Keri looked at her reproachfully. "That is in *such* bad taste," said Keri.

"Sorry!" Lily pulled a face.

"Here's poor Polly, going into anna-wotsisname—"

"Shock," I said. "It's not likely to happen to any of you cos it's quite rare. You have to be extra specially sensitive. But when it *does* happen—" I paused. "When it does happen it's very dangerous. They had to keep me in hospital the whole night."

"You looked death in the face," whispered Frizz.

I said, "Yes, so now I have to wear this bracelet." I held out my wrist for them to see.

"What's it say? Does it say something?"

"Says I'm allergic to insect bites. Mum got it off the

internet. They engraved it specially."

"Cool," said Lily.

"I could have had a pink one. Or one with flowers. Mum wanted me to have one with flowers, but I chose camouflage."

"Yeah, flowers would have been a bit naff," agreed Keri.

"And as for *pink*—"

"Bluuuurgh!"

"This one goes with my combats. I have to wear it *at all times*."

"So people will know what to do if you go into this anna-wotsit shock."

"Right." I couldn't help being just a little bit self-important about it, but after all I was trying to educate them. "I'm going to get a pen, as well," I said. "It's called an *EpiPen*. Then I can jab myself with it if anything stings me."

"Like an injection," nodded Keri.

"Yes. Of course, I'll have to be trained."

"Sounds scary," said Frizz. "Were you frightened, when it happened?"

"Wouldn't you be?" said Keri. "I bet she thought her last moment had come!"

"It would have been," I said, "if Rees hadn't been there."

They fell silent again, thinking about it.

"He saved your life," breathed Frizz.

"It was in the local paper," I said. "Didn't you see it?"

Slowly, they shook their heads. I thought, *well, huh!* So much for fame. Fortunately I'd brought a copy with me. I'd cut it out and put it in my bag, ready to show anyone who took an interest.

"Let's see!" They all edged forward.

"Ooh," said Lily, "you and Rees!"

The man from the paper had insisted on taking a picture of us. Rees had his arm round me and I was scowling. In addition, I was bright red. In other words, *embarrassed*. I'd have liked to have put a paper bag over my head so no one could see me. I think Rees would have done, too. He hates to be in the limelight.

"That is just *so* sweet," said Keri.

"Read us what it says!" Lily bounced back on her cushion. "Read it out loud."

"OK." I cleared my throat. "*When Polly Roberts, twelve and three quarters, and her boyfriend Rees Nicholson, fourteen, took their dogs Rufus and Bundle for a walk across the Downs on Sunday morning and sat down for a rest at the foot of a tree* – it wasn't for a rest," I said. "I was talking to Keri, on the phone – *little did they know they were on top of a wasps' nest. 'It was terrifying,' says Polly, remembering the moment when the wasps came swarming out and attacked them. All four ran for cover, until the wasps gave up and returned to their nest. But Polly had been stung on the arm, and within seconds she was fighting for her life, unable to breathe. 'I thought she was having a heart attack,' says Rees, 'so I tried giving her the kiss of life, but when that didn't work I knew I had to do something. I had to act fast.'* He didn't really say that," I explained. "That's them making things up."

"But he did give you the kiss of life?"

"Yes." I tried not to blush and almost succeeded; just went faintly pink. "I can remember him doing that. I couldn't think what he was doing it for!"

"But it didn't work," said Keri.

"No, cos I was all swelled up. All my throat had expanded. It was like I was suffocating."

"So what happened? What happened?" Frizz was rocking backwards and forwards.

"What happened was..." I went back to my reading. *"With great presence of mind, Rees used his mobile to call 999. 'My first thought was to call my dad,' he says, 'but then I thought it would be better to get an ambulance.' Thanks to this quick-thinking young man, Polly was rushed to hospital and given immediate life-saving treatment. She is now back at home and none the worse for her ordeal. 'But in future,' says her mum, thirty-eight-year-old Donna Roberts, 'she will have to take care and always wear her MedicAlert bracelet.' 'I won't be sitting on any more wasps' nests,' adds Polly.*

Meanwhile, Rees modestly claims that he didn't really do anything. 'Just what anyone would have done.' Polly's mum, however, begs to differ. 'He kept his head and didn't panic,' she says. 'He saved Polly's life. He's our hero!'"

"That is ever such a lovely story," said Frizz.

"Yes. It is." Keri said it almost defiantly, like she was daring someone to contradict her. I'd half expected her to make one of her smart remarks. It takes a *lot* to impress Keri. "Hey," she said, "I remember talking to you on the phone!"

"So it was all your fault," said Lily. "You were the one that made her sit on a wasps' nest!"

"Actually, it was your fault," said Keri, "if you really want to know. I was only ringing to ask how many out of ten she'd give your boyfriend. If you'd've let me meet him, 'stead of keeping him hidden away, I wouldn't have had to ring, I could've decided for myself. So there!"

"How many did you give him?" Lily turned, rather impishly, to look at me.

I said, "Oh! I dunno… Eight? Nine?"

"She gave him *eleven*," said Keri.

Frizz went, "Wow!"

This time, I did blush. I'd sort of got over the worst of my infatuation with Joel – at any rate I wasn't daydreaming about him anymore – but I couldn't help squirming a bit.

"Why won't you let me see him?" demanded Keri.

"You can see him if you want," Lily giggled. "Here!"

She had a newspaper cutting of her own. A picture of her and Joel, doing their *pas de deux*.

"Holy moly!" said Frizz, falling into a mock swoon. "That is seriously high numbers!"

"Could even be a twelve or thirteen," agreed Keri. "Now I know why you've been keeping him to yourself...scared someone'll make off with him!"

Lily looked smug. Over her head Keri mouthed: "*Gay*." I silently sent daggers at her.

"Is he older than you?" said Frizz. "He looks like he is."

Lily said that he was fifteen. "But he's in my dance class cos he only started learning ballet two years ago. Boys often start later than girls."

"Well, that's OK, fifteen is a good age," said Keri. She makes these pronouncements; they are like the word of God. You can't ever argue with them. "Fifteen or fourteen...they are the *best* ages. For us, that is. Sixteen is too old, and twelve is too young. Boys of twelve are *so* immature."

"Darren is twelve," said Frizz.

For just a second, Keri was obviously flustered. She said, "Oh! Yes. Well. Darren." I knew that secretly she'd always thought Darren a bit dull, but not even Keri would be hurtful enough to say so in front of Frizz.

"Darren's different," she said. "Most boys his age are just, like, totally *mindless*. He's more...grown up, somehow."

Frizz eagerly agreed. She said, "It's cos he knows what he wants to do with his life. He has ambition."

"This is it," said Keri.

It occurred to me that up until now she'd probably thought Rees was quite dull, being a boffin and all. But she couldn't anymore! Not now he was a hero.

"Imagine, though," I said, "being given the kiss of life and not being able to enjoy it... Talk about a waste!"

"Even worse," said Keri, "imagine being given it by someone gross and repulsive!"

"Yeeeurgh!"

We all screeched.

"Let's say who we'd like to do it to us if we could choose," said Frizz.

We were back on our favourite subject: boys!

"Go on, then," I said. "You first."

"All right. I'd choose...Darren!" said Frizz, and giggled.

"*BO-RING!*"

"Well, but I would," insisted Frizz.

I thought actually that that was quite brave of her. It made me brave, too. I said, "OK, I'll be boring as well... I'll choose Rees!"

"That's not boring," said Keri, "that's only fair. After all, he did save your life. *Lily?*"

"Not saying!"

"You've got to! You can't get out of it. You'd choose Joel, wouldn't you? You want him to kiss you! She does, she does, she wants him to kiss her! That means he hasn't." Keri mouthed the word again, over Lily's head: *Gay.* "Look, see, she's blushing!"

She was, too. I am always secretly pleased when other people blush, and it's not just me.

"Well, this is all totally uninspiring," said Keri. "And if Lily won't say, I don't see why I should, either."

"I s'pose you'd only choose Damian, anyway," I said. She'd been going on about Damian Whitchurch for months. She'd been so jubilant when she finally got him. "Well," I said, "wouldn't you?" Keri hunched a shoulder. I cried, "Don't say you've gone off him already?" I was only joking; I didn't really think she could have done. Not that fast.

Rather primly Keri said, "Damian and I aren't seeing each other anymore."

"What?"

"Why?"

"What happened?"

We all leaned forward, anxious to hear.

"I thought he was your dream guy," said Lily.

"He was," said Keri, "until he started wanting things

ne couldn't have."

"Such as...what?" said Frizz. I'd noticed increasingly, these days, that she was the one to step in when the rest of us hesitated. She never used to! She used to be quite shy and retiring. Now she is as bold as brass. "What sort of things?"

"Things," said Keri, darkly, "that I wasn't prepared to give."

I wondered what they could possibly be. Not just kissing. I knew she kissed, cos she'd told us, ages ago. Could it be the tongue? I did so want to ask her, but I didn't dare in case it would just be showing my ignorance and I got laughed at.

"Forget about Damian!" Keri tossed her head. "He's rubbish."

"So who are you going out with now?" said Lily.

It was unthinkable that Keri should be without a boyfriend. Sure enough, she wasn't. She'd already fixed another date. A boy in Year 9, who was called Leo, and was "Really cool, you know?"

He was bound to be; Keri wouldn't ever go out with a nerd or a geek.

"So when are we going to see him?" said Lily.

"When I get to see Joel!"

"Yes," Frizz weighed in, very firmly. "Polly's seen him, why can't we?"

"I told you, she's terrified someone'll pinch him!"

"No, I'm not," said Lily.

"Then stop hiding him away!"

"I'm not hi—"

"Yes, you are, don't deny it. Hey!" Keri suddenly sprang up. "I just had an idea! How about we all get together some time? Go out as a foursome? With boyfriends, natch! What d'you reckon?"

I said, "Yes, let's! It'd be fun."

"Frizz?"

"I'm in," said Frizz.

"*Lily?*"

Lily said, "OK. If you like."

"And you'll bring Joel?"

"Well," said Lily, "I don't have any other boyfriend!"

"And she couldn't very well come on her own," said Frizz, as we walked back together afterwards. "So she'll have to bring him! You don't think she's really scared of someone pinching him, do you?"

I said, "No, I think she's scared of Keri telling her he's gay."

"Like she would know," said Frizz.

"Rees seems to think he might be."

"Really?"

We both turned to watch as Lily, in the distance, danced off towards her bus stop.

"You were right," I said. "She's got it really bad."

"I so do not want her to be hurt," said Frizz.

108

"Maybe they've got it wrong! I mean...what does Keri know?"

"Nothing," I said. "She doesn't know anything, she's all talk. And Rees only met him for a few minutes."

"He was probably just jealous," said Frizz. I looked at her in surprise. "Of Joel! Cos of you having a thing about him."

I denied it, indignantly. "I never had a thing about him!"

"He might have thought you did. I thought you did! For a while."

I scowled and said, "Well, I didn't." It was the most terrible lie, and I'm sure Frizz knew it. Maybe Rees had known it, too? Maybe she was right, and he had been a bit jealous?

"Boys *can* be jealous," said Frizz.

I said, "Well, he doesn't have any need to be." That at least was true. *Now.*

It was quite chilly, standing at the bus stop. I thrust my hands into the back pockets of my jeans to keep them warm. "Ooh," I said, "what's this?"

Frizz said, "What?"

"My badge!" The badge that Keri had given me, weeks ago. I'd forgotten all about it. There was just room for it on my lapel between SAVE THE WHALES and HUG A TREE.

"BOYS R US!" I said.

"Could have told you that," jeered Frizz. "You only just found out?"

I gave her a shove. But she was right, of course. A month ago, I hadn't been quite sure. Now I was. Boys were *definitely* us!

MedicAlert

MedicAlert, where Polly gets her specially engraved bracelet, is a charity which provides life-saving identification for people with hidden medical conditions and allergies. You can visit their website at www.medicalert.org.uk

About the Author

Jean Ure had her first book published while she was still at school and immediately went rushing out into the world declaring that she was AN AUTHOR. But it was another few years before she had her second book published, and during that time she had to work at lots of different jobs to earn money. In the end she went to drama school to train as an actress. While she was there she met her husband and wrote another book. She has now written more than eighty books! She lives in Croydon with her husband and their family of seven rescued dogs and four rescued cats.

More Orchard Red Apples